**Hey, TodaysGirls! Check out 2day's
kewlest music, books, and stuff
when u hit *spiritgirl.com***

Copyright © 2001 by Terry Brown

Published in Nashville, Tennessee, by Tommy Nelson®, a division of Thomas Nelson, Inc.

Scripture quotations are from the *International Children's Bible®, New Century Version®:* Copyright © 1986, 1988, 1999 by Tommy Nelson®, a division of Thomas Nelson, Inc.

Creative director: Robin Crouch
Storyline development & series continuity: Dandi Daley Mackall
Computer programming consultant: Lucinda C. Thurman

Library of Congress Cataloging-in-Publication Data

Knowlton, Laurie Lazzaro.
    N 2 deep / by Laurie Lazzaro Knowlton.
       p. cm.
    Summary: Amber needs help from God when she is talked into trying out for the soccer team while being swamped with demands for the Web site she is developing for her school.
    ISBN 0-8499-7680-4
    [1. Soccer—Fiction. 2. Web sites—Fiction. 3. High Schools—Fiction. 4. Schools—Fiction. 5. Christian life—Fiction.] I. Title: In too deep. II. Title. III. Series

PZ7.K7685   00-067880
[Fic]—dc21   CIP

Printed in the United States of America
01 02 03 04 05 PHX 9 8 7 6 5 4 3 2

N 2 DEEP

WRITTEN BY
Laurie Lazzaro Knowlton

CREATED BY
Terry K. Brown

Tommy nelson®
Thomas Nelson, Inc. • Nashville

Web Words

2 to/too

4 for

ACK! disgusted

AIMP always in my prayers

A/S/L age/sex/location

B4 before

BBL be back later

BBS be back soon

BD big deal

BF boyfriend

BFN bye for now

BRB be right back

BTW by the way

CU see you

Cuz because

CYAL8R see you later

Dunno don't know

Enuf enough

FWIW for what it's worth

FYI for your information

G2G or **GTG** I've got to go

GF girlfriend

GR8 great

H&K hug and kiss

IC I see

IN2 into

IRL in real life

JK just kidding

JLY Jesus loves you

JMO just my opinion

K okay

Kewl cool

KOTC kiss on the cheek

L8R later

LOL laugh out loud

LTNC long time no see

LY love you

NBD no big deal

NU new/knew

NW no way

OIC oh, I see

QT cutie

RO rock on

ROFL rolling on floor laughing

RU are you

SOL sooner or later

Splain explain

SWAK sealed with a kiss

SYS see you soon

Thanx (or) **thx** thanks

TNT till next time

TTFN ta ta for now

TTYL talk to you later

U you

U NO you know

UD you'd (you would)

UR your/you're/you are

WB welcome back

WBS write back soon

WTG way to go

Y why

(Note: Remember that capitalization may vary.)

chapter.1

"Come on, Amber! Show me what you've got!" Coach yelled from the side of the pool. Amber's arms burned and stretched as she sliced through the heavy water.

I can do it! Almost there! Her thoughts rushed as swiftly as the water by her side. *Come on. I can do this!* She was going to beat her best time.

WHACK!

Amber's head stung instantly. Her hands flew to the aching spot as if they could somehow massage away the pain. *What on earth?* She felt like she'd hit the wall, but the wall was still ten feet away. She let her feet sink to the floor of the pool. Something bobbed in the water near her. *A soccer ball?*

"Alex, get that soccer ball out of here!" roared their coach. "This is swim team!" Coach Short stomped toward Alex. His ruddy complexion flushed. Amber doubted it was from the sauna-like heat of the pool.

Alex half laughed. "It got away from me," she said. Coach's face remained stern—even Alex knew when Coach meant business. She offered a "Sorry" across the echoing pool.

"Amber, you were really cooking on your time!" Coach called. "Too bad."

Amber's head throbbed from the smack of the ball. "Thanks," she called back. She felt the anger rising inside her. Alex had messed up her best time yet. It didn't really surprise her though.

She should probably be relieved Alex hadn't tossed a bowling ball her way. An image of Alex in her swimsuit, wearing bowling shoes and green-striped tube socks flew into Amber's head.

She smiled and took a deep breath. She thought of the verse she had posted on the Web site that morning, Psalm 90:14. "Fill us with your love every morning." Amber let out a deep sigh. *Lord, fill me with your love, so I can get past this thing with Alex.*

She pulled herself out of the water and scowled at Alex. "What's with the soccer ball?" she asked.

Alex's wavy hair, slicked down by the water, was already springing up. She was the newest member of the swim team. She was a good swimmer, but Amber thought she was kind of haughty. They hadn't gotten along too well at first, but things seemed a little better between them—until Alex did something like bonk her in the head with a soccer ball.

"I'm going out for the soccer team," said Alex. "So's Morgan.

What's it to you?" She dribbled the ball on the wet tile. "My team in Texas made the state finals. I was even voted most valuable player. See, my dad holds the record for . . ."

"Amber," interrupted Coach from behind her. "Did you say you were going out for soccer?"

Amber turned to face him. "Soccer? No way!" she said. Because there was no way she'd join another team with Alex. Even if Morgan was on it. Morgan was Alex's best friend, and the one person who seemed to bring out any good in Alex. *OK, so that wasn't so loving,* she thought. *Try again.* "Soccer's just not my sport, Coach." *How's that, God?* She'd been making a real effort lately to always say the right thing.

"You know, soccer would be really good to keep up your endurance until we start our season. Morgan's going out for it." Coach twirled his whistle. "My wife's coaching the team and practice is right after school."

"Not for me," said Amber. "Thanks anyway," she added, then headed to the locker room.

In first block, Amber sat down just as the morning video announcements began. A neatly wrapped donut lay on her desk.

Zack Huddleston leaned toward her. "Brought some sweets for the sweet," he said, quickly running his hand across his hair. He had a small chunk of hair in front that never went the same direction as the rest of his hair. Amber thought it was adorable.

"Thanks!" Amber smiled. *He's so nice and smells so good.*

"Hey, I didn't get to my Spanish last night," said Zack. "Coach worked us pretty hard. I just went home and crashed. Can you . . . ?" Zack's voice trailed off.

Who could resist that grin? "OK, time for a microwave-Spanish lesson . . ." Amber filled Zack in on everything he never wanted to know about Spanish, quizzing him over their vocabulary list.

"Do you really think we'll ever need to know 'baboon' in *Espanol*?" asked Zack.

"That's not on the list," giggled Amber. "But you might need it if you travel with the football team."

Before Zack could reply, Samantha Moore nudged him and handed him a note. Samantha practically drooled when Zack looked her way. And then she grinned so big, Amber thought the freckles would pop off her face. Zack passed the note to Amber.

Sam arched her dark eyebrows and nodded at Amber. Amber opened the note.

Amber,
    Heard you're going out for the soccer team! You'll be great!
    See you on the field tonight.

                                        Sam

Amber shook her head no, but Samantha was too busy ogling Zack to notice.

4

What's going on? First Coach, now Samantha?

Amber waved to get Samantha's attention. "I don't play soccer. Besides, tonight is my dad's birthday."

"That's very nice, Amber," said Senor Vasquez, perched on the orange stool he sat on during class. "Perhaps we could start today's lesson now?"

Amber could feel her face burn. She couldn't remember the last time she had been reprimanded in class.

"*Triste*, Senor Vasquez," she said. And she was sorry. Sorry that she let stupid soccer get her in trouble.

"Now," said Senor Vasquez. "Don't forget. You've got a test next Monday."

Amber heard Zack groan with the rest of the class. She made note of the test in her day planner, then tried to concentrate on the lesson—not Zack's smile or the curl that rested on his forehead.

When the end-of-class buzzer sounded, Amber scooped up her things and dashed for computer lab. She zipped down the crowded hallway, navigating past clumps of chatting students.

"Hey, Amber!" Sam called behind her. "Wait up!" Sam squeezed through the crowds to Amber's side. Her freckles seemed locked in place again. "You really ought to go out for soccer. Everyone knows you're a great athlete. Give it a shot?"

"No thanks," said Amber. "I have more important things on

my mind than soccer . . . like a gift for my dad. So even if I wanted to play—and I don't—I can't come to practice."

"Don't sweat it." Sam flipped her jet-black hair. "We're only doing conditioning tonight. Come tomorrow night."

Amber couldn't believe it. "Am I speaking Greek or something? I don't play soccer."

Samantha put up her hands. "Whoa. I just thought you might like to do something while swim team isn't competing."

"Sorry, Sam. I'm not myself today." First the hit on the head, then all this in-your-face-soccer on top of worrying about the perfect gift for Dad.

Amber slipped into computer class, headed for her cube, and logged on to her computer.

"Today's the last day for Web master applications," said Mr. Baldwin. He rubbed his head as if to polish it, even though it already shone like a computer screen. "All applications must be turned into the office by 3:00. Edgewood High's Web site goes live September twenty-third."

Samantha raised her hand. "When will we hear the results?"

"Well, the teachers on the committee have to meet and go over the ideas for site designs, and mapping, as well as review the applicants' grades and class participation. We presently have five applications. I noticed you and Amber have both applied. Good luck to you both."

That got Amber's attention. Five applications. Samantha was

in the running. Out of all the students Amber knew, Samantha could be real competition. She was a whiz on the keyboard, pretty artistic, and a good student.

Amber really wanted to be Web master. She had already designed plans for the band and the art students. She'd envisioned the swim team's pages. She'd learned the swing of site construction when she set up the TodaysGirls.com site. Amber and her friends had wanted a private place where they could meet and chat without the worry and sometimes danger of public chat rooms.

Everyone contributed. Jamie created great graphics. Amber's best friend, Maya, kept them all—and their site—state-of-the-art hip with her New York City background. Maya's little sister, Morgan, was all about writing. And she kept them on their toes about the environment. Amber didn't worry too much about the whales with Morgan fighting for them. And Bren was the group enthusiast, a cheerleader through and through. She supplied them with constant morale.

Building the school site wouldn't be easy, but Amber was sure she could make the Edgewood pages rock. She'd spent weeks working on her Web master application. Those busy weeks were the reason she still hadn't figured out what to give her dad.

He'd barely noticed her since he got back from Chicago. They hadn't even gone out for their usual Thursday morning breakfast together. Amber really wanted to blow him away with her birthday gift.

In the lunchroom, the clatter of dishes blended with the hum of conversation. Someone from Zack's table launched a sub-roll into the air. It sailed past the gray walls on a straight coarse for target Lunch Dragon, getting tangled in her hair net. The whole table wailed—till she crammed the tattered sub in a basket with the fresh bread. *Glad I brought my lunch,* Amber thought.

Amber sat down, spilling her lunch sack out in front of her. The others—Maya, Bren, Morgan, and Jamie—were already flipping out over the new Brad Pitt movie playing at the mall. "Have you seen him since he cut his hair? He's an absolute hottie!" Bren's eyes twinkled almost as much as her earrings. She dipped another fry in mayonnaise and shoved it in her mouth.

Beside Amber, Jamie flicked a blob of potato salad off her Levi straight-leg jeans, then tugged her ball cap down over her eyes. "I've heard this movie is supposed to outsell *Titanic,*" she said.

"Get real, girl!" Maya pulled her wire-rimmed glasses off. "Nothing will ever touch *Titanic.* And don't wear your hat so low. I can't see your eyes."

Jamie grinned, took the cap off, and put it on backward. "Is this better?" she asked. Maya shook her head.

Amber's brother strolled toward their table. That soccer ball hit to the head must be causing her to see things. Ryan would rather grow a giant zit in the middle of his forehead than talk to her at school.

"Hey, sis," Ryan called. "Heard you're going to play a real sport. I'll have you kicking goals in no time. Lucky for you, you have me to coach you."

All conversation stopped. Ryan had a way of conjuring silence among groups of girls. Just then Alex showed up and scooched in by Morgan.

"Amber!" Maya whined. "Why didn't you tell me you were going out for soccer?"

"What is it with everyone today?" Amber looked from Ryan to Maya to Alex.

"Well, I'm helping Mrs. Short get you girls playing the game right," said Ryan, pointing at Amber and her friends. "See you on the field."

"You didn't answer my question," said Maya. "Since when do you do something as major as joining the soccer team and not tell me?"

"Honestly!" said Amber. She shook her head. "I am not going out for soccer. I don't know how this thing got started, but it stops here."

Riding her bike home, Amber worried over the gift for her dad. The cool wind rustled the leaves overhead and made her cheeks tingle. She had really searched for a common ground to build on with Dad. Since she was five, Dad had owned the trucking company. Owning your own business could be the pits—it meant a lot of time away from home.

Her father managed to make it to her swim meets. But she knew it was Ryan's soccer games he really enjoyed. Dad had played soccer in college. If it hadn't been for she and Ryan, he'd probably still be playing. That's why she had bought him the book *Bicycles, Bananas, and Breakaway: A History of Soccer*. Amber figured she could read it, too, and then they would have more to talk about. She needed an icebreaker big-time.

As Amber turned her bike into the park, she wondered if maybe she should have gotten him the *Big Book of Crossword Puzzles*. Dad loved crossword puzzles. Amber was definitely more at home with words than soccer. And what if he didn't read the soccer book? She'd be right where she was now with the routine:

"Hi, Dad."

"Hi, honey. How was your day?"

"Great. I got an A on my math test today."

"That's wonderful."

"How was your day, Dad?"

"Good. Busy, but that's good." He'd smile, nodding his head. And then, that awkward silence . . .

Not that her father didn't love her. Amber knew he did. Didn't he come into her room every night, kiss her on the forehead, and say "Love you, pumpkin"? And hadn't she overheard her mom and dad talking about what a great kid she was and how lucky they were that she had a good head on her shoulders?

Well, if worse came to worst, she could just buy the *Big Book of Crossword Puzzles*. Amber rolled into her driveway. Dad was home already. She put away her bike and ran inside. Her mother was running water over a head of lettuce, and her dad was on his cell phone. "No," he said into the receiver, "the shipment has to go out Tuesday." He glanced up at Amber, covered the mouthpiece, and mouthed, "Hi, honey!"

She blew him a kiss and whispered, "Happy Birthday, Daddy."

He smiled. "Thank . . ." But before he could finish, he was talking into the phone again, "This is one of our most important accounts." Amber left the room to knock out her homework. She wanted to finish before dinner so she'd have time with her dad later.

She opened her Spanish book but couldn't resist turning on her computer for a quick e-mail check. There were just a few short notes, one from Jamie about a sculptor she had met at an art show and a longer note from Bren, with a cc to the others about going to the mall.

Work first. Amber started going over her Spanish.

"*Yo hablo.* I speak."

"*Tu hablas.* You speak."

"*Ella habla.* She speaks."

"*Nostros hablamos.* We speak."

"*Ustedes hablan.* You speak, plural form."

"*Ellas hablan.* They speak, feminine form."

Screeeeeeeeeeeech! Car wheels slid to a halt outside. Ryan was home. *Must be close to dinner*, thought Amber. Ryan was never late for a meal. It's like he could smell Mom's cooking from miles away.

"Amber, time to eat!" her mother called.

Amber shook her head, "I knew it," she said, then closed the book and grabbed her neatly wrapped present.

Downstairs, scattered confetti lay on the table, and a huge cluster of balloons fought to touch the ceiling. Mom walked to the phone and took the receiver off the hook. "Tonight's all ours. No phone calls. No interruptions," she said, daring anyone to protest.

Dad smiled and gave her a hug. "OK, honey," he said, turning off his cell phone. "We'll do it your way."

Mom grinned back and winked. This was a real victory. Everyone sat down, then reached across the table to hold hands and pray. Dad bowed his head. For a moment there was silence.

Then Mom began the prayer. Amber knew her mother had hoped Dad would take the lead tonight. But as always, he left it up to Mom. He said Mom was just better at talking to the Lord than he was. Everyone has their talents, he'd say, and Mom had a direct line to heaven.

"Roast beef and mashed potatoes, my favorite," said Dad.

After dinner Mom brought out the cake with a million candles. They flickered then relit each time Dad tried to blow them out. "Don't play tricks like that on an old man!" he laughed.

Amber handed Dad her gift and waited.

"Thanks," said Dad as he ripped the paper off and thumbed through the pages. "I've always wondered how this game got started." He smiled and set down the book.

"You're welcome," said Amber. She twisted a strand of blonde hair around her index finger, hoping Dad hadn't noticed her disappointment.

Next, Mom handed him an envelope with a dinner-for-two gift certificate to Mario's and two passes to the movies inside. "This is from your secret admirer," she said. "Looks like a special date."

Dad kissed her. "Good idea, hon."

"Hey, Dad. You're gonna love this." Ryan handed Dad a gift still inside a brown bag from the store.

Dad pulled Ryan's gift out of the bag. "Great! A hand-held soccer game!" Right away Dad opened the box and started playing.

"Amber, give me a hand with the dishes," Mom said, heading for the kitchen.

"OK, just a minute. Dad, I have another surprise coming for you later," she said.

Ryan patted his hand over his mouth, pretending to yawn. "Are you gonna reenact a scene from your history book?" he asked.

Dad barely looked up long enough to smile, then went back to playing his new soccer game with Ryan cheering him on. Amber's heart ached to be in Ryan's shoes. Standing there, over Dad's shoulder, connected by a game.

Mom took the serving dish from Amber then frowned.

"Amber, what on earth happened to your head?" She pulled back Amber's sandy hair and felt the bump.

"This? Well, Alex got carried away with her soccer ball during Coach's last timing session this morning. She nailed me in the head."

"What was she doing with a soccer ball at the pool?" asked Mom.

"Good question," said Amber just as the doorbell rang.

"Ryan, can you get that?" Mom called.

There was a brief pause, then Ryan's voice yelled back, "Hey, Amber! Alex is here!"

Amber and Mom glanced at each other. It was no secret that Alex and Amber weren't exactly best friends. Mom's green eyes flashed from the doorway to Amber—everyone said Amber had her mother's eyes. "Be nice," said Mom. "I'll finish up in here."

Amber dried her hands and went to the door just in time to hear Alex saying something to Ryan about his help at soccer practice. Dad barely looked up to smile a welcome, and then he was back into his game, absorbed in the zaps, buzzes, and flashing lights.

"Hey Amber," said Alex with her slight Texas drawl.

"What's up?" It had to be something big for Alex to show up at her door. Maybe she'd tried to call.

"Ryan tells me your dad was a soccer great, too. Think you can cut it?" Amber stared at Alex.

"Amber?" interrupted her dad. "You're playing soccer?" Dad

jumped out of his seat, bounded across the room, and threw his arms around her. "This is the best birthday surprise ever! You're gonna play soccer just like your old man!"

Amber nuzzled her face into Dad's flannel shirt. The familiar scent of his cologne mixed with the scent of cedar logs burning in the fireplace. Amber remembered the family ski trip they'd taken a few years ago—the cabin and the snow. Dad had shown her how to build a fire. She really missed spending time with him.

"Yeah," said Amber. "I'm going out for soccer. Practice starts tomorrow."

chapter.2

Amber plunked down in front of her computer. She typed in www.TodaysGirls.com and waited. The screen danced purple and pink, and then "Welcome to TodaysGirls.com" appeared. Amber's Thought for the Day immediately popped up.

Fill us with your love every morning. Then we will sing and rejoice all our lives. Psalm 90:14

Amber read her own written thoughts:

God's gift to us is his love!
Pass it on! Share it! Let it fill your day with joy!

Amber felt like Alex's soccer ball had thwacked her in the head all over again. *Where are my love and joy today? Obviously, God has a plan for me, and now it includes soccer. Didn't God's big soccer plan get my father to jump off the couch and take notice of me?*

OK, God, I'm not going to fight it anymore. I'm giving up my plan of no soccer, for your plan of soccer. Amber keyed in her new verse for the day from Proverbs 19:21:

People can make many different plans. But only the Lord's plan will happen.

Amber began typing her thoughts:

Did you ever start with a plan and God in his persistence turns you around? Sometimes we just don't want to hear him. But God won't give up on us. He has a better plan!

Amber smiled to herself. *I'm going to be a soccer diva. Even Ryan'll be blown away, and Dad and I'll spend lots more time together.*

Still early for the nightly chat, Amber absent-mindedly clicked through the other girls' Web pages. Maya's What's Hot . . . What's Not listed a whole new page of funky earrings, beaded necklaces, and bejeweled bracelets. Only Maya could find the coolest trinkets and trendiest baubles—practically for free—and coach you on how to wear them. No one had an eye for these things like Maya.

Glitter is in--body glitter, glitter nail polish, glitter lipstick, and glittery crystal tattoos! Just don't overdo it. Remember to let your natural beauty shine through too.

Jamie's Artist's Corner had a bio on the sculptor she met at the art show. And she'd listed several sites to view bronze sculptures. Then she ended with a recipe for self-hardening clay.

Amber switched over to Morgan's Feeling All Write. Morgan had a series of poems posted from her classmates on the topic of first love. Then she suggested the readers look up 1 Corinthians 13:4.

Cool! That was a first. Amber had always been the only one to post scripture. *Thanks, God, for blessing me with such awesome friends. I'm glad they're starting to take more notice of you!* Amber looked at the clock and realized instead of being early, she was now late for chat.

She logged in to the room, and her friends' chat names appeared: chicChick, nycbutterfly, jellybean, rembrandt, and TX2step. Amber jumped right in:

faithful1: Hey! Sorry I'm late, wuz checking out pages.
 rembrandt the sculpting recipe is 2 kewl!
chicChick: yeah, I'm making earrings w/ it

nycbutterfly: just don't eat them

jellybean: faithful, when do they announce who's Web master?

faithful1: sometime 2morrow . . .

TX2step: U R going 2 B slammed with 2 sites AND soccer

nycbutterfly: soccer? faithful is so not playing soccer

Amber paused, the reality of her decision about to appear on the screen.

faithful1: who sez changing UR mind isnt a girl's prerogative? Drumroll, please--im going out 4 soccer!

nycbutterfly: ooh girl! u can't kick a football!

TX2step: her dad could have played pro. Ryan's even gonna work w/ the team

nycbutterfly: NW!! im last 2 no :(

faithful1: just decided 2night. U should have seen my dad! it's his best birthday present ever.

nycbutterfly: this I gotta see

TX2step: faithful's dad played in college, just like my dad. she's a natural--even Ryan said so.

faithful1: Coach approves :)

rembrandt: Ha! I get to watch! I M babysitting the boys for Mrs. Short during practices

faithful1: captive audience!

Dropping her fingers from the keypad, Amber made another realization: she hadn't even touched a soccer ball yet!

A tap on her bedroom door grabbed her attention. "Come in," said Amber.

Her dad leaned his head in through the opened door. "Amber, I've got a great idea! How about I pick you up right after practice tomorrow and take you to the mall? You'll need some shoes, shin guards, socks, and shorts for soccer. Doesn't Samantha Moore play soccer?"

"Yeah," Amber said, typing "BRB."

"I thought so," said Dad. "Eric Moore and I used to play soccer together. He's bragged on Samantha more than once. Maybe I'll give Eric a call and see if he and Samantha want to meet us for dinner. What do you think?"

"Sure. Sounds like fun," said Amber.

"Good night."

"Night, Dad."

For a moment Amber just sat there. Her dad was actually taking her out? They were going to spend time together! He wanted to be with her! Who cared if it was to buy soccer stuff . . . whatever that was?

nycbutterfly: earth to faithful1, R U there?
faithful1: sorry! dad just stopped in 2 say good night.
TX2step: did he bring you a glass of water 2?
faithful1: something like that

Amber smiled to herself. Things were working out. All she had to do was play soccer.

> **rembrandt:** I'm outta here. gnosh was busy tonite and I still have homework. C U tomorrow.
>
> **nycbutterfly:** me 2, hey faithful any more surprises?
>
> **faithful1:** No more surprises . . . 4 2day anyway :)
>
> **TX2step:** catch U 2morrow at soccer practice.
>
> **faithful1:** night

At school, Amber checked the announcement board outside Principal Carson's office.

"Bummer," she said to herself. The Web master winner hadn't been posted yet.

Amber hurried to her locker and on to Spanish class. She wanted to look over her homework one more time before class started. She slid past Zack and a gaggle of freshman girls, hanging out in the doorway.

Behind Amber, Samantha wriggled her way past the group. "Hey, Amber. Aren't you the fickle one! Yesterday, no way you're playing soccer, and this morning your dad calls saying we're meeting for dinner after he takes you shopping for soccer stuff."

Amber's face flushed. "What can I say?"

"How about"—Samantha paused, then knocked her fist against Amber's—"Edgewood's soccer team is gonna kick it!"

Amber smiled and nodded. "Yep, we're gonna rock!" But

inside she felt uneasy. *Lord, please help me to be a natural like Dad and Ryan.*

Amber dropped into her desk, barely catching the video announcements for the chatter of the students around her. Senor Vasquez's orange stool was still empty; he was nowhere to be seen. Amber caught random glimpses of Wes Nelson, the junior class president, on the video monitor but couldn't make out what he was saying. His big head just seemed to bob across the screen.

Amber strained to hear what was being said, but there wasn't any mention of the Web master. She ran through her qualifications again. Good student. Top grades in computer class. Experience in building a Web site. A good people person.

What was taking them so long? She had already sketched out several of the pages. Kate Holcombe, Edgewood High's other great artist, and Jamie had given her awesome ideas for the Art Club's page. Amber had even decided which font to use for the school home page. And she had already pulled free graphics off the Web for the Band and Drama Clubs.

Senor Vasquez flew into the room and flung a notebook full of loose papers onto his orange stool. Without a word about his tardiness, he jumped right into the lesson. He raced the class through tenses so quickly that even Amber had trouble keeping up.

"Man, someone had too much coffee this morning," Zack muttered to Amber as they left class.

"Perhaps he was just hungry and hadn't eaten breakfast," Amber responded. "Maybe he didn't get his donut this morning."

Amber hurried down the hall to the announcement board to get a quick look before computer class. Still nothing.

Amber must have checked that board a thousand times during the rest of the day. When last block ended, she headed to the office again. The school secretary sat at her desk, flipping through a stack of files. "Mrs. Wertz, is Mr. Carson available?"

Mrs. Wertz looked up over her glasses, "He's in an area principals' meeting." She motioned toward the closed door. "Is it important?"

"Not really. I was just wondering when he was going to post the Web master results," said Amber.

"I haven't heard. But you applied? That's a big job, Amber," Mrs. Wertz said. She walked toward the file cabinet. "But if anyone can do it, I'm sure you can."

"Thanks for the vote of confidence." Amber smiled.

"I'm sure he'll post it soon."

"Hey, Amber! There you are!" said Alex when Amber walked into the locker room. "Thought you might have ditched us."

Amber shook her head, "No way. I'm here for the long haul." Besides, how could she turn back now? Dad was buying her gear after practice. He'd been so excited about her joining the team. Amber changed into her sweatshirt, shorts, and tennis shoes.

Alex looked her over. "You're gonna need new shoes with

cleats and shin guards," she said, pulling her mane of curls into a tight ponytail.

Amber stared at her old tennis shoes. "My dad's taking me to the mall after practice."

"Go to Soccer Fever," said Alex. "Kind of pricey, but your dad has the bucks to shop there. You'll get by without shin guards today because we're just conditioning. No defensive play yet."

"Mmmm, great!" Amber smiled. *No kicking each other in the shins today! Yeah!*

The next two hours Amber stretched, twisted, turned, ran, and practiced controlling the ball while moving in between orange cones. She felt muscles burn that she had never felt in swimming. On top of that, Ryan kept yelling commands like some kind of he-man drill sergeant. It was enough to make her barf.

"Use both of your feet to get through the cones!" Ryan blasted her as she made her final run through the maze. "Yeah. You can do it!" he said, smacking his hands together in loud claps. "Feel that Thomas soccer gene kicking in your bones!"

Amber swallowed hard. *If I barf, I'm aiming for his shoes. Concentrate. None of this matters. As soon as I get done here, Dad and I are going out together. Without Ryan.*

Amber finished the maze, then flew through the locker room, headed for the shower. Five feet from the stall, a voice stopped her in her tracks. "Rookies shower last."

Amber turned around slowly and saw Alex standing with a towel in her hand. "Just like on the swim team. Remember?"

Amber didn't know what to say. It was true. Rookies showered last. Amber knew because she'd told Alex that same thing when Alex had joined the swim team. And now Alex was telling her? Amber was beginning to like this soccer thing less and less.

Alex's face stretched into a smile. "I'm just giving you a hard time," she said. "Go ahead. You can have my place. I know your dad'll be here soon."

"Thanks," said Amber. "I'll hurry."

Amber raced through her shower and slid her school clothes back on. She peeked out the locker room door but didn't see her dad's truck yet, so she hurried down the hall to check the announcement board one last time.

"Not bad for a first day," Alex said, catching up to Amber. Amber didn't respond. "Did you hear me?" Alex shouted.

"Sorry. I was in another world," Amber said, glancing back at her. *When did my shadow turn into Alex? Be nice. Alex has feelings, too.*

"What has you so bugged?" Alex asked.

"They haven't posted the Web master yet." Amber sighed, waiting for a typical Alex put-down. It didn't come. Through the office window she could see Mr. Carson having a heart-to-heart with a parent.

"Looks like he's in another meeting," said Amber. "Well, I have to go."

"Hey, I have to stick around for a while. I'll check before I leave and catch up with you if I find anything out."

"Really?" Amber couldn't believe it. "Thanks." She slung her book bag across her shoulder and pushed open the door to leave. The autumn sun was already touching the treetops.

"Ready to shop?" Dad yelled out the window of his Ford truck.

"I thought you hated shopping!" Amber smiled, climbing into the front seat.

"Not this kind of shopping." He patted her knee, and they buzzed off for the mall.

An hour later Amber had tried on every pair of shoes in Soccer Fever.

"Isn't this great?" Dad hugged her.

"We'll take the Adidas, this pair of shin guards, and three pairs of the soccer socks." He handed his debit card to the clerk, then looked back at Amber. "You're gonna be great!"

"Thanks, Dad," Amber said. "You really didn't need to buy me those Adidas. I mean, it's a lot to pay for shoes."

"Not for my little soccer champ." Dad hugged her again. The clerk handed him the receipt. "Just in time to meet Eric and Samantha," Dad said.

All the way through the mall to the restaurant to their table, Dad never stopped talking. "Now when you're running down the field and two centers are coming right at you, the best maneuver would . . ."

Amber's mind wandered off to the Web page she could build for the soccer team.

"Hey, Eric! Sam, how are you?" her father asked.

Amber looked up to see the father and daughter standing before her. He had the same dark hair as Sam.

"Here, have a seat," said Dad, pulling out a chair for Samantha. Dad talked sports with Eric while Samantha examined Amber's new purchases.

"Wow! Adidas! These are cool shoes!" Samantha exclaimed.

"I am so pumped you're joining the team," Sam said. "We came close to being a formidable force. We've just been lacking a secret weapon. I think you're going to be the one to put us over the top."

Alex appeared around the corner, trotting toward them. "I found you!" Alex panted. "I know who got the Web master job!"

chapter.3

"T he job's yours, Amber!" Alex squealed. "You are the school Web master!"

"YES!" Amber jumped to her feet. "I am so pumped!"

"Congratulations, honey." Dad lifted his glass of water.

Amber and Alex bonked fists. Then Amber's eyes met Sam's. For a moment Sam's face dropped, but she quickly reached over to shake Amber's hand. "Congratulations, Amber," she muttered. "You'll do a great job."

"Thanks, Sam." Amber shook her hand. "Means a lot coming from you. I'm totally open to ideas, especially yours."

"Well, I do have some thoughts." Samantha's smile returned.

By the next morning Amber had a notebook of ideas for different clubs, sports, and school activities. Zack met her walking into Spanish. "*Hola!* Mighty Web master!" He grinned, and Amber noticed he'd managed to smooth down the tuft of hair on his forehead.

"How did you find out?" Amber tried to act Maya-cool.

"The all-knowing Zack sees everything. I see a beautiful Web master toiling over a large boiling pot . . . no . . . no, not a pot . . . a . . . hmm . . . I have it! A computer!"

"Yes," Amber cooed. "And this stunningly beautiful Web master is designing an award-winning football page."

"Yes, and it has action photographs of its star players, like me, scoring winning goals."

Amber took out her notebook and added Zack's request to her football notes.

"All-seeing Zack, do you know that you are too much?" She sat in her seat. Zack sat beside her, smiling like he'd just scored a touchdown.

"By the way, can I check your homework against mine?" Zack asked. "I wasn't sure about that past-tense stuff we were supposed to do last night."

Amber opened the Spanish book to the page that showed how to change tenses. "I'm not giving you the answers, Mr. See-it-all. The book can do that for you. Look right here." Amber pointed to the spot.

Zack smiled. "What would I do without you?"

Amber laughed. "Why don't you ask your crystal ball?"

Sam slid into the room as announcements began. The first

one came from Mr. Carson himself. "Congratulations to Amber Thomas, our new Web master for Edgewood High!"

Amber couldn't hear anything else after that as her classmates exploded in clapping and calling "Speech! Speech!"

Amber stood, did a play curtsy, and said, "*Gracias. Gracias.*"

"Let me add to your congratulations, Amber," said Senor Vasquez. "Could you stay for a minute after class? I have a few requests for you regarding the Spanish Club's page."

Amber smiled. "I'd be happy to—*Me gusto mucho.*" With that, Senor Vasquez began his lesson. Amber whizzed through the tenses while jotting down an occasional Web site idea.

As class ended, Sam handed Amber a folded note and then zipped out the door:

> Amber,
>
> Coach is looking for dedicated players. Sure hope you don't have any problems managing soccer AND your Web master duties. The final soccer tryouts are on the same day you're to reveal the school Web site. Good Luck!
>
> Sam

For a moment Amber felt uneasy. Sam had always been nice to her. Maybe she was just reading too much into Sam's note. Amber quickly dismissed her worries when Senor Vasquez motioned her to his desk.

"I wrote some ideas down to give to whoever got the Web

master job. I thought perhaps we could have a movie review and perhaps some interviews of students and teachers, all in Spanish. I heard it was pretty close between you and Samantha. I know you will do a great job."

Amber placed Senor Vasquez's requests in her notebook and scurried off to computer lab. Mr. Baldwin had a banner on each computer screen that read, "Congratulations Amber Thomas!" Her classmates inundated her with ideas for the new Web site, and she wrote as fast as she could.

"Chess Club's meetings are held 3:00 to 5:00, with competitions every second and third Thursday." Ethan pushed back coils of dark hair.

"Got it," Amber said, scribbling.

"Do you think you could have a chessboard as a background and the chess pieces moving?" Ethan asked.

"I'll see what I can do." Amber started a second page of chess notes.

"OK, class. Let's get to our seats. Perhaps writing down your requests and giving them to Amber would be the best way to submit your ideas in the future."

"Thanks, Mr. Baldwin. That would be great," Amber said.

Amber took a back table during lunch and tried to sort out the requests she had received. Morgan and Alex spotted her and came to sit down.

"What are you doing back here?" asked Morgan.

"Yeah," added Alex. "Everyone's been wondering where you were."

"I'm hiding," said Amber. "My first day as Web master and look at all the requests I have." She pointed at the stack of papers in front of her.

"Well, save time for soccer," said Alex. "You and Morgan trying out—this is going to be totally cool!"

"Yeah, all of us together!" Morgan took another bite of sandwich. "Speaking of together, I'll grab the others. Maya's gonna be mad 'cause you ditched her."

Just as Morgan got up, a guy at the next table walked over and shoved a note at Amber. "This is from Tim," he mumbled. Scanning the room, Amber spied a freshman boy who looked like he should still be in grade school. He waved at her.

"New admirer?" Alex giggled.

Amber didn't bother to answer. She opened the note:

Web master,

The Audubon club is raising funds for nesting boxes to be placed in the park so we can increase the variety of birds that live there. We'd like to work on an ad to go along with our page. Please inform me of an appropriate time to meet with you.

Tim

Amber looked back down the table at tiny Tim. He tapped his wristwatch, then shrugged his shoulders. Amber thought he mouthed, "What time?" but she wasn't sure. It may have been the lunchroom's fluorescent lights playing tricks off his braces. She wrote on the bottom of his note:

I'll get back to you after I check my schedule.
Amber

Amber passed the note to Tim's table. He gave her a big "OK" sign when he read it.

Amber went back to organizing the Web page suggestions, till Morgan came back with the others. Jamie plopped down on the other side of Alex, and Maya sat down next to Amber. Bren was still clacking across the lunchroom in her newest and noisiest clogs ever.

"This is for you," said Maya, handing Amber a super-chocolate-chewy granola bar.

"Thanks," said Amber. She knew she was lucky to have Maya watching out for her.

The rest of the day wasn't too different from the first half. Everywhere she went, Amber was surrounded by classmates who wanted to talk about the Web site. She couldn't even get away in the bathroom. A red-headed girl she'd never seen before followed her around, asking about a Tae Bo page. Amber didn't know Edgewood High even had Tae Bo.

When the final buzzer sounded, Amber, Morgan, and Alex headed to the locker room to dress for soccer practice.

"Hey, Amber. Wait up!" Zack called from behind her in the hall. He and three other football players strode up to the girls. "We've been talking, and we thought it might be a good idea if you stopped by our practice after school . . . say tomorrow, and saw us in action."

"Yeah! Get some up-close and personal stuff for the Web page," Bear said, striking a pose. Alex rolled her eyes.

"I'll see what I can do. I'll have to work it around soccer practice," Amber said. The three girls filed into the locker room.

"Amber," said Morgan. "Maya would die to be in your shoes. She has a thing for Bear."

On the field, Mrs. Short had already started stretching warmups. Amber found a place at the back of the group and began stretching. She lifted her hands high above her head, took a deep breath, then exhaled. Finally, after being bombarded all day with cyber requests, she felt relaxed.

"OK. Today we're going to zero in on controlling the ball," Mrs. Short shouted. Mrs. Short stood about an inch taller than Coach Short. And she, of course, had quite a bit more hair than him. She usually wore it in a ponytail at school, but Amber had seen her wear it down at church before. Amber's family had known them forever.

"Sam and Alex, please take our rookies through turning with the ball. The rest of you break into pairs and practice tactical tricks like feinting."

"I'll take Morgan, Amber, Kelsey, and Jennifer," Alex shouted.

Samantha nodded and went to work with four other girls.

"What's feinting?" Morgan asked. Amber noticed a large corner of a crispy M&M's package hanging out of her pocket.

"It's faking out your opponent," Alex explained. "You act like you're going to go in one direction, and at the last minute you head in the opposite direction."

"Cool!" Morgan said. She tucked the M&M's back in her pocket.

"OK. Let's run through the cones to begin with." Alex spread out a line of orange cones. "Keep the ball slightly ahead of you so you can see both the ball and the other players on the field."

Amber went first.

"Good job, Amber! You went through those cones like a pro. Morgan, you're next," Alex said. "Amber, work on dribbling with both feet over to the fence while I help Morgan with this."

Amber moved slowly forward, alternating feet and moving the ball ahead in a zigzag pattern over to the fence and back. She tried it again, this time moving in a more fluid motion.

"Way to move!" Coach Short called to Amber. Amber looked up to see Coach standing next to his wife. Jamie wasn't far behind with their boys. She waved at Amber and gave her a thumbs-up. Then she kicked a soccer ball to the boys.

Amber kept practicing. Each time she dribbled the ball, she moved faster and smoother than the time before.

"All right," said Alex. "You and Morgan are really moving well for rookies."

Mrs. Coach called, "Alex! Samantha! Take your groups over to Ryan and start practicing kicks."

"Wait till you see Ryan nail the ball," said Alex. "Amber, if you're half as good as your brother, we're going to be state champs."

"Ladies, may I have your attention?" Ryan shouted.

Alex and Morgan giggled. One of the other girls snorted. *Ladies?* Since when did her brother grow this new attitude?

"Think of the ball as having four prime spots for kicking." Ryan held up the ball and pointed. "One's on the left, two on the right, three in the center, and four low center. If you kick the ball on the left, it will go to the right. If you kick the ball on the right, it will go left. If you kick the ball in the center, it'll go straight ahead and keep low. Kick the ball at low center, it's going to go straight ahead and rise. Now watch."

Ryan called the direction before he kicked the ball, and sure enough the ball did exactly as he said. The eight rookies looked on in awe.

"Way to kick!" Alex bonked Ryan's fist.

"Now let's see what you can do," Ryan said, tossing out a bag of balls.

The rookies spread out and started kicking. Soccer balls flew in all directions.

"Hold it!" Ryan threw up his hands. "OK. Let's try this again. You four start with straight low kicks. You four get the balls back to them. Switch out after the first four have completed five kicks each."

Next time, Morgan's ball zoomed straight ahead, but Amber's ball flew off to the left. On the second round, Amber's ball flew straight and high, landing on the roof of the building.

"Here's another ball," Samantha yelled. "You kicked it too low."

"We get balls up there all the time," said Alex. "The janitor makes a weekly trip up there to clear off the roof."

Amber smiled and kicked again. This time she missed the ball completely.

"Amber!" Ryan yelled. "It helps if your foot makes contact with the ball. Remember the four spots? Aim for the center of the ball." Ryan demonstrated, kicking the ball straight ahead.

Amber felt everyone's eyes on her. She had that sick-grab-you-by-the-throat feeling. She set the ball down in front of her and aimed. *Thwack!* The ball flew off to the right and hit Sam in the side of the head. Amber covered her mouth. "Sorry, Sam! Sorry!"

"Maybe you ought to take those Adidas back," Sam said. "I think they're broken."

The other girls giggled and looked uncomfortable. Amber took a deep breath.

"OK. Switch," Ryan commanded.

Amber fought the frustration building inside her as she ran to get the loose soccer balls. Finally, Mrs. Short called the players together.

"I saw some good footwork out there today. Things are going

to heat up next practice. We only have a short time left until final tryouts. I want to see what you're made of. If you're having trouble in an area, I suggest you do some practicing at home. See you tomorrow."

Jamie and Coach's boys came up to Amber as she walked into the school.

"Hey, you were looking good dribbling," Jamie said.

"Thanks," said Amber.

"Yeah, but you stink at kicking," Coach's oldest son, Harrison Jr., said.

Amber felt like the punch line of a bad joke. It wasn't bad enough she had to embarrass herself in front of the other players and her brother. Now she had a ten-year-old dissing her.

"You just wait," Jamie jumped in. "Amber is always the best at everything. She's going to be Edgewood's new star soccer player."

The boys still looked doubtful. Amber smiled weakly and hurried into the locker room. She tossed her soccer shoes in her book bag. She had a sinking feeling that even a pair of Adidas couldn't fix. For the first time ever, Amber didn't feel the best at anything. She felt like the worst.

chapter.4

Amber flopped down on her bed. *Harrison Jr. was right, she thought. I stink.* She ran through Ryan's lecture again and tried to picture herself kicking the ball like him.

Then she turned on her computer and began searching for soccer sites. She found hundreds—soccer glossaries, equipment, players, news, local teams, and international ones. A cartoon player juggled in the corner of one site. Another site was packed with action shots from high school teams across the country.

She even landed on a page that showed players kicking the ball in slow motion. Amber tried to copy the movements with an invisible ball. She bookmarked that site and kept searching.

The page that really grabbed her attention was dedicated to inside forwards, her dad's position:

Inside forwards are the team's best at speed, dribbling, tapping, passing, and kicking. A forward has to know how to shoot a wide variety of kicks.

Amber's heart dropped. *How am I ever going to play this game if I can't do anything but dribble?*

"Amber!" her mother's voice snapped her back to her room. "Dinner's ready." Amber shut off her computer and trudged downstairs to the kitchen. Just as she walked in, she saw her mom give her dad a quick kiss on the cheek.

"There's my soccer champ," Dad said, folding the newspaper stretched across the table.

"Yeah, she's a champ all right," said Ryan. "You should see her kick." Amber flashed her brother a keep-your-mouth-shut look that he promptly ignored. "Yep, she hit the fence, the roof, and Sam." Ryan laughed.

"Hmm. How about you and me spend some time after dinner kicking the ball?" Dad suggested.

"That'd be great," said Amber, grinning. Ryan looked deflated, and Amber loved it.

When they finished dinner, Ryan helped Mom clear the dishes from the table while Amber grabbed her soccer ball and followed Dad outside.

Dad leaned against the garage door. "You just have to remember if you shoot a bad kick, note what you did wrong. Then think about the right way to shoot that kick. Now go on. Try again."

Amber focused on the ball. *Visualize! You can do it! Thwack!* The ball flew with precision straight at the chalk goal on the garage wall.

"Way to go!" Dad patted Amber on the back. "Now do it again!"

She kicked the ball harder. "Thomas teamwork." The ball hit its mark. "Thanks, Dad."

Later that evening, after she'd showered and worked on her homework, Amber logged on to the Todaysgirls.com site. She watched the computer awaken to her commands. All the others—Maya, Morgan, Jamie, Bren, and Alex—were already chatting. Amber jumped right in.

faithful1: hey gurly girls!

rembrandt: the Web master has joined da room

nycbutterfly: faith--a little bird said ur meeting w/ the football boys 2morrow

jellybean: I don't think a bird told her. I think it wuz a BEAR!

TX2step: a big gnarly one w/ ferocious breath

nycbutterfly: enuf--tex mex--beanie weenie

chicChick: do bears really eat oatmeal?

rembrandt: I think u mean porridge

faithful1: only with tex mex style beanie weenies :)

nycbutterfly: I cant stand this another second!!! how wuz soccer 2day?

TX2step: gr8! 1st scrimmage in a couple of days. the
    team iz startin 2 rock.

jellybean: but mrs coach says we have to wear helmets
    now

nycbutterfly: what????? why????

jellybean: cause faithful keeps kicking people's heads
    w/ the ball

faithful1: do not! it wuz one accident. we do not have to
    wear helmets!

jellybean: teasing

rembrandt: I saw it all. faithful still looked gr8 2day!

chicChick: hey faithful--what happened 2 2day's thought
    4 the day?

faithful1: ahhhh! ive been so slammed. I forgot!

Amber's throat tightened. How could she forget to put up a
new verse? She scribbled a reminder in the notebook with her
Web notes.

faithful1: thanx 4 noticing!

jellybean: soccer wuz a blast 2day. I luv learning new
    stuff

rembrandt: builds character

TX2step: jellybean iz a character already!

faithful1: that gives me an idea 4 a verse

chicChick: here's an idea for cheerleaders' page

faithful1: OK
chicChick: film clips of pep rallies + game cheers
faithful1: I'll add it 2 my list
chicChick: kewl!
faithful1: gotta go be the Web master - - lots to do
nycbutterfly: don't 4get - after school - the football team
   - me and U :)
faithful1: 4get my best bud? NW :) CU

Amber reached for her Bible. *Where's that verse?* She thumbed the worn pages of her New Testament until she found it.

2 Corinthians 4:8–9. We have troubles all around us, but we are not defeated.

We do not know what to do, but we do not give up. We are persecuted, but God does not leave us. We are hurt sometimes, but we are not destroyed.

Are you bummed? Trying your best and getting nowhere? Remember, God is with you. He's your partner. He's there to pick you up and dust you off.

Before going to sleep, Amber flipped through her book of Web site requests. It had grown to encyclopedic proportions. *If I just break the Web site into small pieces, I'll be fine. One group at a time. A-Z. Tomorrow I'll start on archery, art, and Audubon.*

Amber raced through her day planner, writing in days to work on various pages.

She stopped when she got to "S." *"S" is for softball, soccer, and sleep.* Amber turned off her bedside lamp and snuggled under her down comforter. She thought about the time she'd spent with her dad after dinner and fell asleep with his voice in her ears, "Thomas Teamwork! Way to Go! That's my girl!"

The next morning Amber felt renewed. She had a plan of attack. *This is gonna be a good day. Just keep it positive. After all, I'm athletic. I studied the soccer Web sites and practiced with Dad last night. I just started off on the wrong foot.*

She laughed at herself. *That's good, the wrong foot . . . kicking. OK, so it wasn't so funny. Think positive. Not humor. Today I'm going to kick that ball like a sharpshooter! They'll put my name in the Hall of Fame.*

At school Amber was again bombarded with Web page requests. "I had no idea there were so many groups, clubs, sports, classes, teachers, or people in this school," Amber said to Maya as they walked past the library.

"Yeah, now you're the center of attention!" Maya smiled. "Nobody even notices *me* anymore."

"Even the cafeteria ladies gave me suggestions today." Amber ignored her friend's sarcasm and pulled the list from her notebook.

"You've got to be kidding me!" Maya straightened her leather skirt.

"No, really. They want the menu posted. And they thought it would be nice to highlight one personality from the food staff each week."

"I can see it now." Maya laughed as they pressed through the masses. "This is the Dragon Lady. She eats seniors for lunch every day."

"Sweet." Amber laughed. "Speaking of sweet, don't forget our date with the football team."

"Get real, girl!" Maya rolled her eyes and shook her head. "I'll see you after class."

Amber barely listened to the day's final lecture. She spent most of class organizing the latest Web site requests and sketching preliminary page designs—fonts, color, and placement of photos. She needed to check with Mr. Baldwin about using the school scanner.

When the final buzzer sounded, Amber packed her notebook. She met Maya in the hall outside her door.

"You ready?" asked Amber.

Maya glanced down the long hall. "Have you seen Morgan and Alex?" she asked. "Are they coming?"

"Not that I know of," said Amber. "Why would they?"

"Morgan begged," said Maya.

Amber was surprised. It wasn't that Maya didn't want to be around her baby sister. It was just that her baby sister was always with Alex, and Maya did try to stay clear of Alex.

"They must've changed their minds," said Maya. "Or mind,

rather." She smirked slyly and tucked a chunk of dark hair behind her ear, revealing a silver hoop earring. "I didn't think you'd care, and it doesn't even matter now."

Amber locked eyes with her friend. "What are you talking about?" she asked.

Maya took a deep breath. "It's really nothing," she said. "Alex has a crush and won't tell Morgan who it is. So Morgan figured if it was one of the football players, Alex would tag along today. But since they haven't shown up, it looks like it's not one of the football guys."

"Oh," said Amber. Between soccer practice and her Web master duties, Amber had enough to worry about. She wasn't terribly concerned with Alex's love interest.

"Okay then," said Amber. "Let's go. I only have a half-hour until soccer practice, so let's go see what these guys are up to."

Amber and Maya wove their way through throngs of students to the weight room. The smell of sweat and rubber mats hit Amber head-on. Everywhere she looked, football players lifted weights and worked out on machines. Amber felt like she was at a circus packed with strongmen. Only none of these guys had mustaches.

Zack set down his weights with a thud. "The almighty Web master has arrived!" he announced. His teammates stopped exercising and swarmed Amber and Maya like paparazzi. Maya was all smiles. Amber knew she was eating it up.

"I don't have long," said Amber. "So let's get started. How

about you all sit down and share some thoughts on the football page?" Amber directed. The guys eased back and sat down as if she were holding court, while Maya kept a running dialogue with Bear.

"Who's first?" Amber asked, pulling out a legal pad and pen.

"I'd like to see game highlights," Jack said. His shirt looked like it had been doused with lime Gatorade. He stood six foot high and was as solid as a pillar of the White House.

"And what about a player of the week?" Zack asked.

"We could have a weekly contest," Chris, a freshman bench-warmer, shouted. "You know, like *Who Wants to Be a Millionaire.* Only it could be like *Who Wants to Be a Football Player?* And we could have football trivia questions, and . . ."

The guys threw towels and plastic water bottles at Chris. He shielded his head with his arms. "You gotta stay with the trends!"

"Right, Chris," Zack said, patting him on the back. "You just keep thinking, buddy." Zack shot one of his million-dollar smiles at Amber.

"How about some photos of us working out?" Bear flexed his muscles.

Maya let out a squeal. "Love it!"

Amber narrowed her eyes at Maya. All of a sudden, the guys started flexing and posing and slamming chests together, grunting, "Oh, yeah!"

Amber cleared her throat. "Gentlemen, I'm on a clock here. Can we get back to business?" The football players looked like five-year-olds who'd just run out of Halloween candy. They plopped back down on the mats.

"To answer your question, Bear," Amber shouted, "it might be cool to have a few—I repeat, a few— shots of what you guys go through to become the undefeated team that you are." Bear puffed up his chest like a rooster. Maya fanned herself in response.

"You know what I thought would be funny?" Joe asked. Amber couldn't imagine what Joe was going to come up with. He had been a prankster since she'd met him in seventh grade, and he put a whoopee cushion on Miss Simpson's chair in English.

"We make mock mascots for the other teams. Before the game you could post the mock mascot on the site! Like this week we play the Brighton Bulldogs. We could get a bulldog and dress it in a pink tutu."

Everyone laughed. "That is too funny!" Maya leaned into Bear.

"Or like the Creston Cowboys," Chris shouted over the laughter. "We could rope a cowboy!"

"How about a pirate ship in the bottom of a fish tank and say, 'Sink the Pirates!'" Zack yelled.

"I know," Bear said. "For the Wadsworth Hornets, we could have a picture of a giant fly swatter with our school name on it, smacking a hornet."

Amber frantically wrote down the ideas while Maya laughed with Bear over the giant fly swatter.

Amber turned when she heard the door beside her open. It was Bren. She burst into the weight room, the clear rhinestones spelling "cheerleader," glittering across her pink tank. "Are you fellows still hogging the weight room? The cheerleaders need to start their workout."

Amber glanced at her watch. "Ack! Soccer practice starts in three minutes!'"

chapter.5

Amber flew out of the weight room and headed for the girls' locker room. *How am I ever going to change clothes and be on time? I'm never late to anything, and all of a sudden I'm either cutting it close or actually late. Me late!*

"Amber!" Principal Carson rushed up and blocked her from rounding the corner. "Do you have a minute?"

Amber slid to a stop. "I'm on my way to soccer practice."

"This will only take a minute." Mr. Carson searched his sports coat pockets.

A minute's all I have. She bit the inside of her cheeks, willing him to get on with it.

"First of all, I haven't had a chance to congratulate you for being appointed as the school Web master." Mr. Carson pulled out a wallet-size black leather notebook.

"Thank you." Her eyes wandered to the clock ticking away behind Mr. Carson's head. *This is going to take forever.*

"I had some thoughts about some of the things that might be good additions to the Web site." He opened the notebook and pulled out a list.

Amber took a deep breath. *Good. A list. Just hand me the list and let me go.*

Mr. Carson began reading. "I think the Web page should include safety information, such as fire drill rules, exit doors, tornado procedures, posture and safe shelter spots in case of a tornado, security protection of the student body from these threats. You know, things like that."

"Sounds great, Mr. Carson." Amber reached for the list. "I'll take the list and look it over."

Mr. Carson kept reading. "I also thought we should have an alumni page. This is a place where Edgewood alumni could have a Hall of Fame for our alumni who have achieved greatness out in the real world. They could have announcements for things like weddings, births, and, sad to say, deaths. It could be a great tool for public relations in our community and beyond."

Amber glanced at the clock. Five minutes late, and she still had to change. "Cool idea, Mr. Carson."

He smiled. "There are plenty more where those came from."

Amber smiled back. "How about I stop by your office and we can brainstorm? I'd hate to miss anything." *Anything like soccer practice.*

Mr. Carson nodded. "You're right. Let's meet tomorrow."

"Tomorrow sounds great!" She dodged around him and slipped away to the locker room. Amber threw off her clothes and pulled on her shirt, shorts, and soccer shoes. She glanced at the clock as she ran to the field. Thirteen minutes late.

"Amber, nice of you to join us!" Sam shouted.

Mrs. Short eyed her watch as Amber walked up. "Amber, give me thirteen laps."

Amber started to protest. "I'm really sorry. I . . ."

"Sorry doesn't cut it. Run!" Mrs. Short turned to Morgan and tossed her a ball.

Amber sprinted to the track. *How on earth did I get myself into this mess? So, God? When do you pick me up and dust me off?*

As Amber jogged, she watched the other girls dribbling, kicking, and defending the ball. Alex and Ryan worked with some of the rookies. Ryan acted as goalie, his regular position, and Alex showed the rookies how to try to get a scoring kick past Ryan. Good luck. Amber had seen the best of the best try to score on Ryan. His height, long legs, and sure hands made it almost impossible to get past him.

Amber fought to control her breathing as she rounded the track for the eleventh time. *Breathe in. Breathe out. Breathe in. Breathe out.* Off to her left she caught sight of Samantha cheering on Morgan for cutting past her opponent.

Amber's legs tightened and cramped as she struggled around the track for the twelfth time. From the corner of her eye, she saw Alex rush at Ryan, then kick the ball past him into the net. Amber stopped short.

She knew Alex was good but to get past Ryan? Had he let Alex score? The rookies were going wild whistling and slapping Alex on the back while she strutted across the field. Ryan shrugged his shoulders as if to say, "Hey, it happens."

Amber thought she'd seen everything, but Ryan letting a girl score on him was too much. She finished her last lap. Her nostrils burned. She felt like she had an elephant sitting on her chest as she crossed the field.

"Amber, I want you to join Samantha's group." Mrs. Short barely looked up from scribbling on her clipboard.

Amber bent over, gasping for air. She lifted her arm to say "OK" and headed toward Sam's group.

"Trap the ball with the sole of your foot. Like this." Sam's legs moved like a well-oiled machine. "Use the inside of the foot."

The rookies tried forward position, dribbling the ball—passing it to the person next to them. The ball snaked back and forth between the players.

Amber looked back at Sam. "Looks like you're going to be practicing with me." Sam bounced the ball on her knees. "Think you can do it?"

Amber sucked in a deep breath of air and nodded. Sam dribbled the ball, and Amber kept pace, running along beside her. *Thwack!* Sam passed to Amber. Amber tried to trap it, but the ball bounced off her foot and flew toward the other rookies.

Sam shook her head. "Try again."

Amber's brow glistened from running. *Visualize trapping that crummy ball.* Again, Amber kept pace with Sam. This time when Sam passed the ball, Amber trapped it. Yes! She never lost step but just kept moving with the ball, and then she kicked it back to Sam.

"Way to go, Amber!" Alex called, jogging over while clutching two balls. "We've come to change groups. You guys come with Ryan and me to work on kicking goals."

Amber and Morgan swarmed with the other rookies to where Ryan stood waiting.

"Girls, we're going to show you why knowing where that ball is going matters." As he talked, Ryan toed the ball, alternating feet, keeping the ball in the air.

"Alex, try to get something past me." He fixed his eyes on Alex.

She shuffled the ball, took aim, and shot. Ryan flew through the air like a Roman candle and stopped the ball.

"That, girls, was a Lofted Instep Kick. Again!" Ryan ordered.

Alex advanced toward Ryan. This time she lifted the ball with the tip of her toe and carried it with her instep. It flew high toward the goal, but Ryan scooped the ball out of the air.

"Good example of a Chip Kick," Ryan said. "Just not good enough." He grinned. "Hit me with your best shot."

Alex maneuvered the ball, faking to the right side of the goal. Ryan mirrored her. Then at the last minute she shot a low drive to the left. It flew past Ryan and into the corner of the goal.

Alex jumped. "Yes!"

"And that, girls, is your best bet to get past the goalie." Ryan picked the ball out of the net. "The low drive to the corner is one of the toughest balls for a goalie to stop."

What was this, the Alex and Ryan Show?

"OK," said Ryan. "Give it a shot."

Morgan was first up. Her face looked pinched. She darted forward, mimicking Alex, then aimed and kicked three times but nothing got past Ryan.

With each of Morgan's shots, Amber visualized kicking the ball. *A center kick sends the ball straight and low. A kick on the left side sends the ball to the right. A kick on the right side of the ball sends it to the left. A kick to the bottom center sends the ball high and straight. I can do this. I can send this ball right into the goal.*

"Amber, you're next." Alex rolled the ball to Amber.

Amber trapped the ball and dribbled toward Ryan. She watched her brother match her step for step. Taking aim she kicked the ball with a strong instep kick.

Ryan stuck out his foot and stopped the ball. "Good try. Bet you can't do it again."

Amber gritted her teeth. "Watch me."

She dribbled the ball, picturing it sailing past her brother. But instead, her foot sailed over the top.

"You missed!" Ryan doubled over in laughter. "I can't believe you missed it!"

Alex covered her mouth with her hand. "Hey, it happens. Try again."

Amber felt a knot the size of the moon growing in her stomach. The other rookies stared and smirked. Sam's group walked over to join Amber's group. Ryan crossed his arms and rapped his fingers impatiently against his biceps.

Amber gulped and dribbled the ball toward Ryan. He didn't even look her way. *Focus on the ball, not Ryan.* She aimed and shot. The ball flew off to the right, nowhere near the goal.

Ryan looked up. "Are you going to shoot that ball or what? Oh, you already did." Then he laughed. Sam rolled her eyes.

The knot in Amber's stomach grew to the size of ten moons. Alex rolled Amber the ball again. *Visualize. You can do this.* But all Amber could visualize was her brother laughing, Sam rolling her eyes, and Alex trying not to crack up.

Amber dribbled toward the goal, took aim, and kicked. The ball skirted off to the side, falling short. Her face stung. Inside she was crumbling. *I hate soccer.*

Alex retrieved the ball and rolled it to Haley. "OK, Haley. You're up."

Amber stood off to the side, not wanting to make eye contact with anyone. She heard her father's voice in her head: *Visualize what you did wrong, visualize doing it right, then move on.* But Amber could never get past what she'd done wrong.

Mrs. Short blew the whistle, and the players circled around her.

"Well, ladies, I saw some great things happening out there today. You just might make a decent soccer team yet."

"She must not have seen Amber," Sam said under her breath but loud enough for Amber to hear.

"Tomorrow is our first scrimmage," Mrs. Short reminded, flipping pages on her clipboard. "I've broken you into two teams. I've mixed the teams with seasoned players and rookies."

Sam groaned.

"I've done this for a reason. I want to see you girls pull together as a team. The rookies will excel to the seasoned players' levels, and the seasoned players will need to work harder to win."

Mrs. Short studied her list and brushed a loose hair away from her face. "Alex, I'm putting you in charge of A team. Sam, I'm putting you in charge of B team. Cassi Williams, A team, Jennifer Stark, B team. Molly Anderson, A team. Amber Thomas, B team…"

When Amber's name was called, she saw dread on Samantha's face. Mrs. Short read on through the list of names. Amber watched the girls on Alex's team gather together, patting each other's backs and knocking fists.

Sam scowled at Amber. When Mrs. Short looked up from her list, Samantha buddied up with one of her new teammates and acted psyched. But as soon as Mrs. Short's gaze moved back to her list, Sam's scowl returned.

"See you in the morning," Mrs. Short finished up. The players headed for the locker room. Amber jogged to the front of the crowd through groups of chatting girls discussing soccer, classes, and boys. Amber grabbed her clothes and shoved them in her book bag. She wanted to get out of there as fast as she could.

But before Amber could slip out, Sam stepped in front of her. "Listen, Amber. I already lost Web master to you this week. I don't plan on losing this soccer game, too. So, I suggest you figure out how to kick a ball or call in sick tomorrow."

chapter.6

"Amber!" Mom called. "Wes is on the phone."

Amber took the call in her room. "Wes, what's up?" Wes, the junior class president, never called Amber unless he needed something.

"Hey, I was wondering if you'd like to get a burger at the Gnosh and talk Saturday?"

Amber hesitated. The last she'd heard, Wes was still going out with Cassie Williams. "Sure. What do you want to talk about?"

"Well, I've been thinking about prom." Wes paused. Amber tried to conceal the sound of her breath as it involuntarily drew in sharply. Wes continued, "And the Web site. I think we could really do something cool to promote it. I'd really like to talk it over with you."

Amber sighed. She should have known. "OK. What time?"

Hours later Amber stared at the home page she'd developed for the school. She liked the way she had offset the photograph of Edgewood High and incorporated the school colors—purple and gold—and the mascot, a giant eagle. Her eyes hurt, and her back ached. But Amber felt like she'd finally done something worthwhile.

Unlike soccer. How could she play soccer tomorrow? Sam had ordered her to call in sick. That would sure be the easy way out. Not having to humiliate herself in front of half the world.

But it's not the world I'm worried about. It's Dad. Maybe if I don't tell him about a scrimmage tomorrow morning . . . I could keep practicing . . . just hold Dad off until I can kick that lousy ball where I want it to go . . .

She pulled up the TodaysGirls Web page and read her latest verse.

> **When I suffer, this comforts me: Your promise gives me life. Psalm 119:50**

Amber had always liked that verse. She read on through her Thought for the Day.

> **Are you hurting? Are your parents on your case? Or are you having trouble in class? God wants to wrap you up in his loving arms. Let him!**

Amber skipped on to her e-mail. She had a message from Maya.

Hey girl!--
I'm so psyched! Bear and I had the best time on our date
tonight. IM me first thing in the morning for all the
details.

--Maya.

Amber chuckled. Maya would probably start with what Bear wore. His wardrobe looked like something from a fashion magazine. Maya relished sharing every moment from start to finish. She never left out even the littlest detail—whether he opened the door for her or pulled out her chair at dinner or helped her with her coat. Maya knew chivalry was alive and well.

Amber woke up at 6:15 even without the alarm. She felt nervous and anxious about the scrimmage. *Lord, I need to feel you beside me today. Please fill me with your comfort.*

Amber knew Maya wouldn't be online yet, so she went straight to work on the school Web pages. She built a cyberspace outline of pages with the suggestions she pulled from her notes. She could add colored backgrounds and different fonts later, when she placed the photographs, moving pictures, and sound. Right now she just needed to take this Web site one step at a time.

Amber could hear her house awakening. She checked the clock—8:10, time to see if Maya was on IM yet. She wasn't, so Amber left her an e-mail:

NYC--
Can't wait to hear about your date with Bear! Guess what? Wes called yours truly. At first he acted like he wanted to ask me for a date to prom. (He actually said the p-word.) But then he said he had some ideas to use the Web site to promote the prom. So typically Wes. He did ask me to go out and get a burger and talk. Anyway, I have a scrimmage this morning. Call you when I get home.
--Amber

Amber showered and scrambled for breakfast. Ryan was already mowing down a mixing bowl full of Wheaties.

Amber lifted the empty box. "Hey, you ate it all!"

"Wouldn't do you any good," said Ryan. "It's the breakfast of champions, and we both know that's not you."

"Ryan, you're a champion jerk." Amber grabbed a bagel and left the kitchen.

She threw her shoes and a soccer ball in her bag. She didn't need to be at school for another forty-five minutes, but she thought she could get some practice in before everyone else showed up.

"Where are you off to this morning?" Dad asked as she unlocked the front door.

" I'm . . . I'm," Amber sputtered.

"She's off to her first scrimmage." Ryan stood in the kitchen doorway.

"Amber, why didn't you tell me?" Dad asked, his eyebrows knit together.

"No big deal." Amber cleared her throat. "It's just a scrimmage. I figured you were busy."

"I'm never too busy to come and see one of my kids play soccer!" Dad grabbed his jacket from the hall closet.

For the second time that morning, Amber felt like someone had knocked the wind out of her. Dad came to swim meets sporadically at best. Now, in the name of soccer, he could drop everything? Her emotions swirled in her head like water down a drain.

"Great, Dad," Amber managed. She opened the door. A blast of cold air took her breath away.

"Wait! I'll give you a ride!" Dad followed her out.

"Dad, why don't you meet me there?" Amber turned and tried to smile at him. "The game doesn't start for another hour and a half. I'm just going early to do some Web site stuff." Amber hated using the site as an excuse to keep her dad away— hated to lie—but she needed time on the field to herself.

"OK. I do have a few things I should do this morning." Dad put his keys back in his jacket. "See you there."

Amber jumped on her bike and pedaled like her life depended on it. By the time she got to the school, her legs were cramping. She parked her bike and tried stretching the cramp out.

"Morning, Amber! You're early!" Mrs. Short shouted. She stepped out of her Accord. "I like that in a player."

Amber shrugged. "I really need to practice without the pressure of someone watching."

"Let me know if I can help," Mrs. Short called, heading to the locker room. "I'll be out later."

"Thank goodness." Amber sighed. First, she worked the kinks out of her legs. Then she proceeded to dribble and kick the ball at the goal. Time after time, she dribbled and kicked. With each kick, Amber felt impending doom. The ball had a mind of its own.

Amber stopped as other players began showing up. She jogged into the locker room to get a drink of water. When she came back, she saw her dad pull into the lot. Ryan and Alex poured out of the front seat. What was Alex doing in her dad's truck?

Amber trotted over to them.

"Thanks for the ride," Alex called over the truck to Dad. "Hey, Amber! Ready for the big scrimmage?"

"As ready as I'm going to be." Amber glanced at her dad and saw him frown.

"This should be good." Ryan smirked.

Mrs. Short whistled the players to the locker room for a pregame speech. "I know you girls are good. Show me how good you can be on the field today! I'm watching to see how you do under pressure. Final cutoffs are coming up quick. Make me believe you're a soccer machine!"

The players exploded out of the locker room to warm up. Amber stretched, dribbled, and practiced passing the ball with Morgan. Finally Mrs. Short blew her whistle to call them to their positions on the field. Amber scanned the crowd in the bleachers as she trotted to her position as halfback. Her dad sat beside Sam's dad. Maya and Bren cheered down in front.

Maya hated soccer. Amber thought how lucky she was to have Maya as a best friend. Jamie was running around after the Short kids. Coach Short paced along the sidelines, arms crossed while his wife shouted last-minute instructions.

"Here we go," Amber muttered as she fidgeted with her socks.

The whistle blew. The ball flew, and players exploded in motion. Samantha wriggled through the crowd with the ball. Amber stepped ahead with her teammates while Samantha swiveled this way and that, the ball an extension of her foot. Amber watched, trying to look like an active part of the team. *Lord, please let me look like a player, and please don't let the ball come to me.*

On the sidelines Samantha's dad yelled louder than anyone else. "Take it all the way, Sam!"

Amber glanced over to see her dad cheering right beside Mr. Moore, both standing in the bleachers. Sam sprinted ahead, aimed, and kicked a goal. Instantly players mobbed her with congratulations.

The ball was returned to the center circle, and with the kickoff, the opposing teams sprinted into motion. The ball was intercepted, then intercepted again. Then the thing Amber dreaded the most happened—someone passed the ball to her.

She watched the ball whirl to her like a magnet to metal. *I can do this. Just dribble toward the goal.* She tapped the ball then moved swiftly ahead.

"Way to go, Amber!" Dad called from the sidelines.

Suddenly a player from the other team moved in and tackled. Amber struggled to keep her footing, and the player tore the ball away and headed downfield. Morgan scrambled after the ball, but the lead was too big. The other girl took aim and made a clean shot and scored.

"Let's pull together!" Sam called to her teammates. "We can't let them get the ball!"

The rest of the game seesawed. Amber's team scored, and then the opponent's team. Amber always managed to be the last person on her team to touch the ball before the opponents stole it and scored.

Sam came up behind Amber and snarled, "I thought I told you to stay home!"

Two minutes left, and the game was tied 5 to 5. The kickoff sent the ball toward Morgan. She dribbled it forward and passed to Amber. The opposing team's Full Inside Forward dogged Amber, trying to steal the ball again. Amber struggled to keep the ball clear of her opponent.

Whoosh! Amber felt a hand on her back, then she stumbled. The referee blew the whistle and awarded Amber a direct free kick.

The crowd in the stands jumped to their feet. "Amber! Amber! Amber!" they chanted. She heard Bren's voice above everyone else's.

Taking her position directly in front of the goalie, Amber inhaled. *Visualize. Keep it low and deep.* She could feel all eyes on her. The clock counted down 26, 25, 24. Amber aimed and kicked. A hush fell over the crowd.

The ball flew. The goalie dived and caught it, then kicked it back into play. The center from the other team got the ball and dribbled down the field. The clock continued counting down 7, 6, 5 . . . The center kicked the ball. The ball slipped past the goalie. Score!

The clock ran out. The opposing team erupted into cheers. Final score, 6 to 5.

"You blew it! We had the game, and you blew it!" Sam's face flushed red.

From midfield, Amber watched her father. *I let him down. He gave up his time to see me lose the game for my team.*

Mrs. Short called the team together on the side of the field. "That was some good playing out there. A very lively game. I can see we definitely need to work on defensive plays and field-goal kicking."

Amber's insides flipped. She knew their coach was talking

directly to her. "Now remember. I'll post our soccer team list next Monday. At the game next Saturday I'll be watching for players who can control the ball, play defensively, and shoot the ball where they want it to go. With the information I have so far and the results of next Saturday's game, I'll make the final cuts."

Amber's dad was waiting for her in the bleachers. Sam's dad was still beside him, waving his hands in all directions as he talked. Mr. Moore was probably bragging about how great Sam played and teasing Dad about what a loser Amber was.

"I'll see you all Monday at practice, regular time," Mrs. Short said, as she gathered her clipboard and stat sheets.

"Or not," Sam mumbled. "Why don't you go back to swimming, Amber. You're not doing the soccer team any good."

"Back off, Sam!" Amber threw her bag over her shoulder and stormed away from the group.

Maya, Bren, and Jamie were waiting for her by the gate.

"Hey! Great game!" Bren shook her blue fleece scarf like a pompom.

"Where were you?" Amber asked. "I lost the game for my team."

"It's only a game," Maya said. "Why don't you quit if it bugs you that much?"

"Because I'm not a quitter." Amber walked through the gate. "Besides, there isn't anything I can't do if I set my mind to it."

"Sorry! I forgot who I was talking to." Maya stepped back. "Switch gears—let me tell you about my great date with Bear!"

N 2 Deep!

Amber leaned against the fence, wishing she could be more like Maya. She might obsess about food and fashion, but she'd never freak about kicking a ball, that's for sure. Amber smiled warmly at her best friend.

"OK, so like Bear comes by at like 7:00. Exactly at 7:00. Not late. Not early. And he looked so fine."

Jamie and the boys kicked the ball against the wall beneath the bleachers. "Talk louder so I can hear!" she shouted.

Maya raised her voice. "And we went to the movies with some of the other jocks. But they were being rejects, so Bear says, 'I don't what to share you with these boneheads,' and we moved. Isn't that just too cool! And then we . . ."

Maya went on for what seemed like hours, and Amber's mind wandered off to what her father was probably thinking about her.

"Are you listening to me?" Maya asked. "Earth to Amber!"

"I heard you," Amber said. "Bear rocks, right?"

"Tell me about Wes's call." Maya leaned against the bike rack.

"Oooh, Wes called you?" asked Bren. "He is so hot!"

Morgan and Alex walked up. "Who's hot?" Morgan asked.

"Wes is." Bren winked.

Mrs. Short came around the corner to collect her boys from Jamie. "Thanks for watching them." She ruffled Harry Jr.'s hair.

"No problem," Jamie said, but Amber had helped sit for the Short boys and knew they were usually a problem. Mrs. Short and her boys vanished inside the Accord.

"Come on! Tell us about your date with Wes!" Bren looked like she was ready to burst from the suspense.

"There isn't much to tell." Amber glanced at her dad, and he waved toward his truck. "Just we're going out to get a burger tonight, and we're supposed to talk about prom."

"Hmmm," Maya cooed. "Maybe you and Wes and Bear and I could double to the prom?"

"Maya, you are so not even hearing me." Amber waved back to her dad and pointed at her bike. "I'll meet you at home," she called. Dad nodded back to her. Amber turned to Maya again. "You and Bear are like a couple, and Wes and I are class officers, OK?"

"Whoa, girl!" Maya backed off. "I was just saying there's more to life than stupid soccer, like the prom, and boys, and I don't know . . . life! So get over it!"

"Maybe you're right." Amber unlocked her bike. "Sorry."

"Hey, no prob." Maya grinned. "Talk to you later."

"Sure." Amber rode away. She knew nothing was going to let her forget even one minute of the game, the look on her father's face, or her own disappointment.

chapter.7

Amber pedaled home slowly. She wasn't anxious to get there—to see her dad or hear Ryan. *Dad probably thinks I'm a total spaz—a loser. And in front of Mr. Moore, too. What's wrong with me?* The embarrassment burned her eyes. *I'm not going to cry! Don't cry.*

She rode up her drive and saw her dad's truck wasn't there. *He probably went to check on things at work. Or maybe he's avoiding me.* She could feel the lump in her throat growing.

She raced to her room, then jumped in the shower. No sooner did she turn on the water than she let the tears flow. *God, I know you have a plan. Dad and I are spending more time together. Alex and I aren't fighting. Please, God, help me be good at soccer for Dad's sake. Don't let me embarrass him again.*

Amber dried her hair in front of the mirror. She had her dad's smile, so why couldn't she have his soccer talent? "Quit bumming." She spoke sternly at her reflection. "Do something positive!"

Amber jumped into working on the school Web site. She plugged in the type fonts and page backgrounds she had envisioned the night before. Engrossed in her work, she didn't hear her dad come in until he stood behind her.

"Wow! That's impressive." Dad leaned over her shoulder and squinted at the band photos on the screen.

"You think?" She turned to face him and saw the soccer ball tucked under his arm.

"I was wondering if you wanted to go and kick the soccer ball around some?"

Amber knew what he was really saying: Man, do you need to practice! "OK. Let me save what I have here. Be right down."

She shut off her computer and headed downstairs, wishing she and Dad could do anything except play soccer—even change the oil in his truck.

When Amber got outside, she saw Alex there talking with Dad in the driveway.

"Hey, Alex. What's up?"

"Left my shoes in your dad's truck." Alex looked freshly showered, with new jeans and lipstick. "What have you been up to?"

"Still working on the school site," Amber said, coming up alongside her dad.

"Quite impressive from what I saw." Dad bounced the soccer ball to Alex.

"You ought to see the TodaysGirls' site," Alex said. "It's really cool."

"Thanks," said Amber. "I've been meaning to make a few additions but just haven't had time lately."

"Where's your brother?" Alex asked, glancing around.

"We're going to work out without Ryan to hassle us." Amber passed the ball to Alex. "Want to join us?"

"Can't. Maybe next time." said Alex. "I promised Gramps I'd help him with some stuff around the house."

When Alex left, Amber and her dad practiced defensive plays. Dad modeled tricks to avoid opponents. "A good way to get away from the player who's marking you is to pretend to kick the ball, but place your foot on top of it like this."

Dad demonstrated the move, faking a kick. "Then, using the heel of your foot, roll the ball behind you, like this." He pushed the ball behind him then whipped around and moved off in the opposite direction. "The key is to do it fast so your opponent is outmaneuvered."

After working Amber on defensive plays, Dad marked the side of the garage with a chalk goal. "This is how I learned to kick goals. Shooting soccer balls off your grandparents' garage." He worked with Amber the rest of the afternoon, guiding her through an array of kicks.

"Well, I'd say you're showing some real progress," Dad said when Amber stopped to catch her breath.

"I've still got a long way to go," she said, feeling a blister burning into the back of her heel.

"You'll get it!" Dad winked. "You're a Thomas. Thomases have soccer blood flowing in their veins."

Amber nodded, wondering if the soccer genes might skip a generation in girls.

"Phil, phone!" Amber's mom called out the kitchen window.

Dad kicked the ball square into the chalk goal one last time. "I knew they'd be after me sooner or later." He shrugged. "You've got what it takes, Amber," he added and patted her back. "Just bring it out."

Amber practiced until the shadow of the house stretched long across the driveway and she realized it must be time for Wes to come over. She'd just finished brushing her hair when she heard the doorbell ring. Dad answered the door. She could barely make out the conversation as she hurried down the stairs.

"Yes, sir," Wes said. "School's going great."

She hustled to the living room. "Hi, Wes." Wes was wearing a brown nubby-wool sweater with jeans and black boots. Maya would approve.

Wes, Amber, and her dad chatted for a few minutes until she and Wes made their getaway. Amber slid into Wes's '79 Chevy with leopard-print seats. The engine roared over the country western music blaring from his speakers. *Who would have thought?* Amber pulled the seat belt snugly around her.

"So this is the real you?" asked Amber, eyeing the hula dancer on the dash.

Wes smiled. "One side of me anyway," he said. "You're lucky it's Saturday. On Tuesdays I drive a pink golf cart." Amber laughed.

The Gnosh was packed—typical for a Saturday night. Jamie flew around like she had on in-line skates.

"Hi, Jamie!" Amber called as Jamie weaved between tables, a pitcher of Dr. Pepper in one hand and a tray of Gnosh burgers in the other.

"Hey, girlfriend!" Jamie shouted. "I'll have a table for you in about five minutes."

Sure enough, just a few minutes later, they slid into their booth. Wes glanced at the menu then got down to business. "Amber, I know you're into the Internet, but do you have any idea about the power of Net advertising?"

"I guess." Amber shrugged, looking over the menu she knew by heart.

"I'm telling you the Internet and advertising go together like foot powder and ripe shoes. Like fried bologna and white bread. Like —"

"I get what you're saying," interrupted Amber. She wrinkled her nose.

"Right," said Wes. "We need to promote the prom on the school site. It's so clear!"

Amber had never seen Wes so passionate.

"I just know if you set this up right, we'll surpass all past proms," he continued. "I want this prom to go down in history as the best bash ever held by Edgewood High."

"I'm with you on this," Amber reassured him. "I've got some great graphics in mind."

"But graphics won't do it! I really think we need to sell tickets online!" Wes banged his fist on the table to stress his point.

"Boy, Wes." Amber squirmed in her seat. "I don't know about that."

"If we want a good size crowd, it makes sense," Wes countered.

"I don't think Mr. Carson's gonna go for selling anything."

"You have Carson wrapped," Wes said, shedding his jacket. "You can do it. Selling prom tickets over the Internet is gonna put us over the top."

Amber could see Wes really wanted this. "I'll see what I can do," she said.

Jamie suddenly popped up beside their table. "You guys ready to eat?"

"Yeah." Wes handed the menu to Jamie. "I'd like a Gnosh Deluxe and a Dr. Pepper."

"Got it," Jamie said. "Amber?"

"Chicken sandwich and a vanilla shake." Amber winked at Jamie.

"Did you hear about Craig Wilson?" Wes unwrapped his silverware. "Remember when Mr. Carson got on the PA reminding students about the no tolerance rule for public display of affection? Craig walks into the lunchroom with AFFECTION written in big red letters on a poster board. The Dragon Lady asks him what he's up to, and he says . . ." Wes started laughing.

Amber leaned forward, waiting for the punch line.

"He says, 'I'm publicly displaying affection.'"

"No!" Amber nearly choked.

"Oh yeah. The whole lunchroom burst out laughing. The Dragon Lady never even smirked! She just wrote him up. Everyone started booing and telling her to lighten up." Wes shook his head. "Man, the whole scene almost caused a riot."

They talked right through dinner and on until the Gnosh emptied. But when Wes dropped her off, he reminded her to get the ticket sales past Mr. Carson. Amber said she'd try.

"Amber!" Mom called. "Amber, are you up?"

Amber sat straight up in bed. "What?" Music blared from her alarm. "Amber?" Her mother walked into her room. "Didn't you hear your alarm?"

"No," said Amber rubbing her eyes. "I never heard a thing until you called."

"Do you feel OK?" Mom felt her forehead.

"I'm fine," she said. "Guess I zonked out."

"Hurry and get dressed, or we'll be late for church," Mom said as she left.

Amber raced around her room. She pulled on a black cashmere

sweater, red-and-black plaid skirt, and black stockings. Her mother had an English muffin all buttered and jellied for her to eat in the car on the way.

People were still filing into church when the Thomas family sat down. Amber let the choir music wash over her. The sound always seemed to speak to her soul. But when the talking started, her mind sometimes wandered. Church service proceeded, but Amber hardly noticed.

Then all of a sudden she heard, ". . . you will find rest for your souls. The work that I ask you to accept is easy. The load I give you to carry is not heavy."

Rest. Right now she needed God's rest. *Lord, I do have a heavy load—I feel like I'm being sucked up by soccer, school, friends, and the Web site. I'm not doing all this for me. I'm trying to fulfill your plan. I'm just trying to make my dad happy. I'm trying to make everyone happy with their pages on the Edgewood Web site.*

The closing song brought Amber back to the moment. She walked outside with her family, the fall air blowing leaves in circles around the parking lot.

"Good morning!" Coach Short called. Mrs. Short was swinging arms with Chris, while Harrison Jr. and Nat ran circles around her. Coaching soccer must have been easy compared to raising her boys.

"How's soccer going?" Coach Short asked.

Before Amber could say a word, her father jumped in. "She's doing fine. We've been doing some extra practice."

"I'm working at it," Amber said quietly.

The Chandlers joined them in the parking lot. "Amber, how did your date go with Wes last night?" Jamie asked. "You two practically closed the Gnosh with me."

Amber smiled. "It wasn't a real date. Wes just wanted to talk about using the Web site to promote prom."

"Sure." Jamie lightly pushed Amber. "I saw you two laughing."

"Wes is a good storyteller," Amber said brushing her hair out of her face.

"Wes is a pretty boy," Ryan interrupted.

Jamie rolled her eyes. "Talk to you later on chat."

On the drive home, Amber's parents talked about taking a vacation to New York for Thanksgiving.

"I've always wanted to see Macy's parade and shop at Tiffany's." Mom smiled over her shoulder.

"Yeah, but doesn't a long ski weekend in Colorado sound more relaxing?" Dad gave Mom a pleading look.

Ryan jumped into the conversation. "Oh yeah! I need to learn how to snowboard! What better place than Aspen?"

"Amber, what do you think?" Mom was obviously fishing for support. Dad parked the car, and everyone piled out.

"Both ideas sound cool," Amber said.

"Whatever, little Miss Kiss-up," Ryan muttered as he passed her up.

Amber stuck her tongue out at her brother and went to her room. She had more important things to spend her energy on—

like a Spanish test, the school Web site, and most of all, learning how to kick that stupid soccer ball.

She read through her Spanish, reviewed her vocabulary words, and practiced changing tenses. She didn't hit her books as hard as usual, but she knew the material well enough. She could feel the clock ticking, and she still had to do pages for the basketball team and the chess club.

She'd need to spend every spare minute working on the site to get it done by the end of the week. But before tackling that project, she went to the TodaysGirls site and updated the verse and Thought for the Day. She decided to use the verse from church, Matthew 11:29–30:

Accept my work and learn from me. I am gentle and humble in spirit. And you will find rest for your souls. The work that I ask you to accept is easy. The load I give you to carry is not heavy.

Do you ever feel like life's got you by the arm, dragging you along? God offers a getaway. Give him the heavy stuff.

Amber reread her comment, then clicked back over to the school site. She was totally immersed when someone knocked on her door.

"Amber?" Alex slipped in. She had on her gym pants.

Amber swung around in her chair. "Alex!"

"I was wondering," Alex said, "if you wanted to kick the ball around."

Amber hesitated and then said, "Sure. I've been sitting here for a couple of hours. It'd feel good to move around."

"Hey, maybe Ryan would play goalie for us?" Alex suggested.

"Yeah, right!" Amber said, tying her shoes. "He'd rather play dead on the couch."

Amber and Alex started out working on defensive plays. Then they moved on to dribbling and passing. Finally, Alex had to go home. But Amber still felt keyed up. She dribbled to the side of the garage and practiced kicking.

She kicked the ball again, and again, and again. The night sky faded from orange to gray, and she still kept kicking. *I am going to conquer this sport. I'll show them all. Amber Thomas can't be beaten by a soccer ball.*

chapter.8

Amber was digging through her purse for her Chapstick when she heard Mr. Beep, Maya's Volkswagen Beetle, in the driveway. Amber jerked on her shoes and swept through the kitchen, grabbing a piece of banana nut bread as she ran out the door.

"Hey!" Maya said. She had on her new red peacoat.

"Good morning!" Amber piled in the car, her bag crowding her feet. "Want half of my banana nut bread?"

"Ew! Bananas shouldn't even *be* in bread!" Maya cried. "It's greasy and gross—and I'd just have to floss again with walnuts stuck in my pearly whites."

"Your loss," Amber said, munching off a corner. "This is great stuff."

"How about if I treat the soccer star to a real breakfast?" Maya asked, backing out of the drive.

Amber glanced at her watch. "I can't be late. I've got a test this morning."

"I'll get you there on time." Maya winked at Amber. "Trust me. It'll be fun."

"All right," said Amber. "And I'm no soccer star. More like a soccer crater. Or a big black hole."

Maya pulled into Pat-a-Cake and hit the curb before coming to a stop. "Whoa, Mr. Beep."

"Man, this place is packed," said Amber.

"I know." Maya gave one of her devilish grins. "The football team's here."

Amber climbed out of the car. "What am I gonna do with you?"

"Thank me." Maya's red boots clicked across the pavement. She grabbed Amber's arm and pulled her inside.

Everywhere Amber looked, football players filled the seats and stood in the aisles.

"There they are!" Maya maneuvered her way through the crowd to Bear and Zack. Amber followed close behind.

Bear stood up when he saw Maya. "Hi, sweet thing!"

"Bear!" Maya tilted her head. "You're too nice."

"Hey, Amber!" Zack flashed his perfect smile. "I've been thinking more about the team's Web page." He handed Amber a chocolate-covered donut with cream filling oozing out both ends. "We could have a pregame and postgame chat." Zack bit into a twist roll, barely chewed, then gulped it down almost whole. "The pregame would be great to get us pumped. We could talk about our strengths and what to expect from the other team."

Bear chimed in. "Why did the Raiders cross the street?"

"I don't know," Maya answered. "Why?"

"To get away from us!" Bear spiked an imaginary football. Several teammates chanted, "We bad! We bad!"

Maya laughed. "OK. How about this one? Knock! Knock!"

Bear answered, "Who's there?"

"Betcha," Maya said.

"Betcha who?" Bear asked.

"Betcha we're gonna beat-cha!" Maya cracked up at her own joke.

The football players jumped up. "We're number one! We're number one!"

"See!" Zack applauded Maya and Bear. "Amber, this is great stuff." Maya and Bear took a bow.

"Fans could get online for our pregame build up. This Internet thing is gonna rock."

Amber felt herself carried along by the crowd. She loved that they were into it. "That's a great suggestion. I'll see what I can do." But inside, her little voice didn't agree with what her mouth was saying. She'd never have time to do all this.

"Amber is a genius!" Maya put her arm around Amber. "You won't be disappointed."

Amber glanced at the clock. "Bell rings in ten minutes. We have to get out of here."

"Honestly, you're going to give yourself an ulcer," Maya said. "We have plenty of time."

Patricia, the owner of Pat-a-Cake, banged a pot and pan together. "Officer Manning will be here in three minutes. If you kids aren't out of here by then, he's going to close me down for exceeding patron capacity."

Patricia had a loud bark and a soft heart. Nick, one of the line-backers, climbed over the counter and lifted the woman right off the ground. "Thanks, Mom!" He planted a big kiss on Patricia's cheek.

"Aw, get out of here before I report you all for bein' truant." Patricia swatted her son with a towel.

Everyone filed out of the bakery laughing and yelling. They formed a caravan and headed to school. Amber flew through the halls, sliding into class just before the bell rang. Zack waltzed in behind her.

"Zack," Senor Vasquez said. "You're lucky I'm in a good mood this morning. I'm giving you a warning. Perhaps, next time I'll mark you late."

"*Gracias!*" Zack saluted Senor Vasquez.

"OK, clear your desks for the quiz." Senor Vasquez pulled a pile of papers from his briefcase. "You may begin as soon as you receive the test." He walked around, handing out the test papers, and checking to see that students had their desks clear.

Amber wrote her name at the top of the test and began. She plodded through each question, taking her time, and checking each answer twice. Then she came to a vocabulary word she didn't know. *The Spanish for "baboon"? I thought Zack was kidding. This wasn't in my notes.* Amber looked up. Several students were already done, sitting with their papers turned over, staring off in space. *Maybe I just read it wrong?* She looked at the question again. *Nope. Why don't I know this?*

Amber moved on to the next question. *OK. Just one question. I'll go back to it.* She answered the next three and then hit another word she didn't know. *I should have read over the chapter better.* She glanced up again. Senor Vasquez was looking around to see if everyone was done. Zack sat with his hands folded. Amber raced through the next few questions. *Why didn't I study more?*

"Put your pencils down and trade papers with your neighbor," Senor Vasquez said.

Amber felt sick. *No! I didn't finish!* She clutched her paper.

"Is there a problem, Amber?" Senor Vasquez asked.

Amber shook her head and handed her paper to Zack. She couldn't even swallow. *Two answers I didn't know and three I didn't finish. That's five. Five wrong. Maybe more?*

Senor Vasquez went through the answers, question by question, calling on people. Everyone seemed to know the answers. Even Zack answered one.

"The grading scale goes like this," Senor Vasquez said. "Fifty questions, each question is worth two points. Do the math. Then hand the pages back to their owners."

"Good job, Zack." Amber passed back his quiz. "You got a ninety-four."

"I beat you!" Zack said loud enough for everyone to hear. "I got a better grade than Amber! She only got a ninety!"

Amber's face burned. Not only was this her first non-A, but Zack was making a major issue of it to the whole class.

"Amber got a ninety?" Sam repeated. "Zack, maybe you ought to let me coach you with your Spanish. I got 100."

Amber wished she could disappear. She searched for a good response. "Everyone has an off day." The buzzer sounded, and Amber jumped out of her seat like it was on fire.

"*Adios!*" Senor Vasquez stacked the papers on his orange metal stool.

Amber fled the room with Sam on her heels.

"Seems like your off days happen more often than not," Sam said softly. "Maybe you've bitten off more than you can chew. Maybe you should give up something, like say . . . soccer."

"Just worry about yourself, Sam," Amber said, forcing a Maya-cool grin. "I'm doing fine."

"I don't know," Sam said, matching Amber stride for stride. "There are A players, and there are B players. I think we know where you are."

Amber tried to shake Sam as they turned down the hall past the sophomore lockers, but she kept after her like a mosquito.

"Of course you could wait until cuts," Sam said. "Then you could be embarrassed in front of everyone. 'Amber Thomas dumped from the team.'"

Amber stopped right in front of Sam. "You know what I

think? I think you're afraid I'll make the team and pass you up. Then where would your claim to fame be?"

"Oh yeah. I'm real worried about that!" Sam snapped.

Amber turned and stormed into computer lab. Before she could even put her books down, Mr. Baldwin asked, "How's the Web site coming along? Are you gonna have it up on time?"

Amber forced a smile, stuffing her feelings from her fight with Sam. "Sure. I worked on it most of the weekend."

"Good." He held out a stack of odd-sized papers. "Here are some more requests."

Amber took the papers and stuck them in her notebook. "Thanks. I'll work on these tonight."

The whole time Amber worked on her computer, she wished she were at home. She'd rather be tweaking the school Web site than doing the everyday stuff they were covering in class.

Plus, she felt bombarded. Everywhere she turned, someone shoved a request in her face. If she were stuck on a deserted island, a bottle would float up with some new idea in it: Hey, Amber. Can you make a scratch-and-sniff page for the Fungus Club? She knew all she really had to have was a great home page and a sampling of the clubs and sports. But she wanted the site to blow them away.

After class Amber raced down the hall to switch books and pick up her lunch. As she neared her locker, she slowed at what looked like a mob scene.

"There she is!" Tim from the Audubon Club shouted, pointing at Amber.

All off a sudden the mob of students swarmed her like bees out for blood.

"Amber, the Arts Club should go first on the Web site," Kate said. "After all, we do start with A."

Nick Russo, captain of the basketball team, glared down at her from a foot above. "Amber, the basketball team wants equal time with the football team. We heard you're doing a before-the-game chat and an after-the-game chat, personal interviews, and—"

"Amber," William, the second-chair trumpet with a voice deeper than the ocean, interrupted. "When are you installing the band sound clips?"

"Amber!" Lindsay shoved a tattered script in Amber's face. "Drama Club's play begins October second." Lindsay waved her hands around in the shape of a two while holding up two fingers. Amber thought she could lay off the interpretive dance long enough to speak. "We need advertising space now!" said Lindsay. Amber blinked at Lindsay, wishing she could turn her into a billboard.

The buzzer sounded, and just as suddenly as the swarm had attacked, it dissipated.

"Saved by the bell," Amber muttered. She decided to skip the possibility of a lunchroom mob and headed for the one place on campus where she knew she could find peace—in the water.

The stillness of the pool reminded her of God's serenity. She breathed deep the familiar smell of chlorine and humidity.

Suddenly all she wanted to do was swim. Amber walked to Coach's door and knocked.

"Amber, what can I do for you?" Coach leaned back in his creaky desk chair.

"Coach, I really need to swim." She almost choked on the words.

Coach hesitated for a moment, then said, "OK. Make it quick. I have a meeting in twenty minutes, and you can't be in the pool if I'm not back here."

Amber threw on her suit and dived into the water within moments after asking. The water wrapped her up and washed away the stings of the morning. With every stroke, she could feel herself renewed, stronger. God was her partner. He had a plan.

I can get through this. Stroke. *I'm willing and able.* Stroke. *I won't be overwhelmed.* Stroke. *God has a plan for me.* Stroke. *The school site's gonna rock.* Stroke. *Everyone will love it.* Stroke. *I can accomplish anything I set my mind to.* Stroke. Amber pushed herself, swimming her stress into oblivion.

Coach blew the whistle, bringing her back. "That was some good swimming. Wish I'd been timing that."

She pulled herself out of the pool. "Thanks, Coach. I really needed a swim."

"Do you want to talk?" Coach stared at her, eyebrows arched.

"No, thanks," said Amber. "I've got everything under control."

Amber climbed out of the pool with a plan.

chapter.9

Amber knocked on Mr. Baldwin's door. "Excuse me."

Mr. Baldwin swung around in his chair. "Well hello, Amber. What can I do for you?"

"I was wondering if I could come in before school and during lunch to work on the school Web site?" she asked.

"Sure you can!" Mr. Baldwin pulled off his glasses and polished them with a threadbare white hanky from his back pocket. "I've been waiting to see how I might be able to help you. I didn't want to step on your toes."

"Thanks, Mr. Baldwin. I really appreciate it." Amber sat across from his desk.

"You know you can use anything we have to make the site a winner," Mr. Baldwin said.

"I was hoping you'd say that." Amber took out her notepad. "I'm going to need to use the school scanner."

"No problem. You've used the school scanner here in class." He patted the large white scanner on his desk. "It gives a nice, clear, crisp picture."

"Thanks!" Amber flipped through her notes. "Band and choir want sound clips. That takes up so much memory and requires a lot of time to download."

Mr. Baldwin's face scrunched up in thought. "I'll help you create a hyperlink to a sound file instead. That way the visitors to the Web site can decide if they want to take the time to download and hear the clip."

Amber slapped her forehead. "Why didn't I think of that?"

"You know," Mr. Baldwin said, biting on a pencil. "You could work on this in class, too."

"Thanks. I may need to if I'm going to get it done by the twenty-third."

The next part of Amber's plan had to wait until after soccer practice. She went through the day feeling more like her old self—in control, ahead of the game, ready to take on the world. Even soccer practice went without embarrassment. She managed to stay clear of Sam's and Ryan's venom and even shot a few good kicks.

After practice she waited for Ryan by his locker. "I need to talk to you."

"What do you want?" Ryan checked out two senior girls as they walked by.

"I need you to make me a soccer star." She waited for the abuse she knew would follow her request.

Ryan didn't disappoint her. "Yeah, right. And I want you to make me the President. Face it, sis. You're a soccer spaz. Swim, yes. Soccer, no. Loser. Total loser."

"Exactly," Amber agreed. "The great, the cool, the awesome Ryan Thomas's sister is a loser. So what does that say about Ryan Thomas?"

"That he's coordinated and his sister is a wimp?" Ryan cocked his head.

"No." Amber set her plan in motion. "It says that 'Ryan can't possibly be as cool as we thought he was. Look at his sister.'" Ryan's head snapped around. Amber knew she had his attention now. "Yep, like sister like brother. Loser."

"I'm no loser," Ryan said, glancing both ways, probably making sure no one heard him say the word *loser.*

"Maybe, maybe not." Amber headed home. "But I heard some girls from the team talking and . . ."

"And what?" Ryan grabbed Amber by the arm.

"Well, let's just say they were beginning to wonder about your status on the school's 'coolest' ranking." Amber jerked her arm free and began walking away, leaving Ryan to simmer in shock.

"Gotcha," Amber muttered.

"What did you say?" Ryan demanded.

"Meet you in the driveway!" Amber called. She'd hit her mark.

As soon as she got home, Amber started kicking the ball against the garage.

"You're doing it all wrong!" Ryan yelled as he walked up behind Amber. "How many times do I have to tell you? The ball is broken into four parts."

Amber tossed him the soccer ball. "So walk me through it again."

Amber worked with Mr. Baldwin on the Web site all week. She watched the pieces come together—pictures, sound, and script. Soccer, on the other hand, didn't come together. She could picture the moves in her mind, but her body didn't follow.

Thursday after practice, Alex walked home with Amber. "You want to run defensive plays again?" Alex dribbled the ball.

"All right." Amber was tired, but she knew she had to get her moves right if she wanted to make the team. Amber tapped the ball from her left foot to her right then tried to kick it past Alex. Alex intercepted the ball as Ryan pulled into the drive.

"Maybe Ryan will play goalie today?" Alex suggested.

"You'd have better luck winning the lottery," Amber muttered. Alex kicked the ball, just missing Ryan as he climbed out of his car.

"Alex! Are you trying to kill me?" Ryan stopped the ball in midair and rolled it back.

"We could use a goalie." She kicked the ball straight at Ryan again.

"You really think you girls can get anything past me?" Ryan smirked.

"I've done it before, and I'll do it again!" Alex challenged.

"I let you score as an example for the others," Ryan countered.

"Yeah, right." Alex turned her back on Ryan and passed the ball to Amber.

Amber watched stupefied as her normally aloof brother threw off his jacket and jumped in front of them.

"OK." Ryan motioned with both hands. "You get five shots each!"

Alex and Amber worked together dribbling, passing, and kicking. But Ryan always stopped the ball.

"Time for a break!" Amber's mom called from the kitchen window. "Warm cookies." Ryan raced inside with Alex and Amber following behind.

"A mother who makes homemade cookies?" Alex said. She folded her arms and leaned on the gray countertop.

Mom gave Alex the first cookie. But before Mom could pass the plate to Ryan, he had already snagged and devoured two. "Slow down, Ryan." She handed him a glass of milk. "You're going to choke."

Ryan grabbed three more oatmeal raisin cookies and chugged down his milk. He brushed the crumbs off his shirt onto the black-and-white-tiled floor below.

Mom's signature oatmeal raisins weren't Amber's favorite, but she'd never tell her mom. The recipe had been handed down from generation to generation.

"Amber?" Mom held up the plate.

"I'll pass for now. Thanks."

"You've been working yourself so hard out there," Mom insisted. "Come on. Have one of my famous cookies."

"OK," Amber gave in. "Thanks, Mom. You're the best."

"At more than cookies—and don't you forget it." The phone rang, and Mom answered it. "It's Dad," she said. "He made it safely." She took the phone into the den.

"I think you're playing much better," Alex remarked, picking raisins out of her cookie. "Don't you think so, Ryan?"

"Sure." He laughed, and milk dribbled from the corner of his mouth.

"I don't know." Amber sighed. "I'm afraid I'm going to blow it on Saturday and not make the cut."

"Are you nuts?" asked Alex. "You're way better than half the rookies at dribbling and passing."

"Yeah, but I still can't kick the ball where I want it to go." Amber turned off the oven. Her mom must have left it on by accident.

"Well you can't score if nobody dribbles or passes. Right, Ryan? And you're not bad at avoiding tackles, feinting, and passing. Don't you think so, Ryan?"

"I guess." Ryan grabbed the last cookie. He had a raisin stuck between his top front teeth.

"Just get the ball down the field and pass it off to someone who can shoot." Alex stared at Ryan's mouth. "That's what being a team is about. Working together. Uhhh. I think there's something on your teeth, Ryan."

"I'm outta here." Ryan tossed the napkin toward the trash can and strutted off.

"What's with him?" Alex looked hurt.

"He's a toad! And he's my brother!" Amber glanced at the kitchen window then threw the rest of her cookie into the trash. "You want to work some more?"

"Nah, I have to get home," Alex said. "My grandparents are probably throwing a fit wondering where I am."

After dinner, Amber bounced upstairs to check her e-mail and update her Bible verse and Thought for the Day. She had a few minutes before the TodaysGirls chat, and so she put her head down on her desk to rest a minute.

She woke up hours later with key marks on her cheek, and a school of fish swimming by on her screen saver. She looked at the clock. Two-thirty in the morning. The house was silent. *Dad must've left town,* she thought.

If Dad had been home, he would have come in to say good night. He would have seen her crashed out on the keyboard and made sure she'd gotten to bed. Amber crawled under her comforter, missing her dad.

God, please watch over my dad and bring him home safe. She yawned. *And God, please make me a good soccer player so I can make*

Dad proud of me. Thank you, God, for all your blessings, my family, my friends . . . But before she could finish, she was sound asleep again.

Friday morning Amber got to school just behind the janitor. She'd had trouble embedding the cheerleaders' video clip into the site, so she wanted to try again. Mr. Baldwin helped her solve the problem, but she still struggled with the download time.

On the soccer field that afternoon, Amber jumped into the workout to relieve the pent-up tension from the day. She'd started feeling better about her kicking when Mrs. Short called the girls together.

"You'll be on the same teams as last week," she announced. "I'll be looking for teamwork along with skill."

Sam raised her hand. "Mrs. Short, I thought you taught us that we're only as strong as our weakest link."

"That's right, Sam." Mrs. Short didn't look up from her notes.

"Then why are you putting rookies on the same team as some of the more seasoned players?" Sam demanded.

"Because I'm still evaluating our new talent," Mrs. Short said. "These scrimmages don't count on our season record, and they allow me to see what our rookies can do."

Amber knew what Sam was up to. Sam wanted Amber off her team. Amber's throat tightened. *Lord, help me not to feel this way.* She gathered her things and headed for the locker room.

"Don't let Sam get to you," Alex said, following her in. "She's a worm."

"She's afraid I'm going to lose the game for her again," Amber said, struggling to get her confidence back.

Alex opened her locker. "You're so much better than when you started."

"Yeah, I used to stink. Now I'm halfway decent." Amber threw her shoes into her bag.

"You're way better than halfway decent," Alex said. "You were doing pretty good last night."

"Thanks, Alex," Amber said. *So weird. Who would have thought Alex would ever go out of her way to make me feel better?* "You're OK, Alex."

"Yeah," said Alex. "You're not too bad yourself."

Morgan dragged into the locker room and sat on a bench in front of the lockers.

"I'm tired, too," said Amber. "I probably won't even make it to the Gnosh tonight. Will you tell Maya I'll call her later?"

Morgan nodded. "I think she's going out with Bear anyway."

Walking home, Amber prayed. *God, I'm trusting your plan. Help me keep my act together to get through all this. I'm grateful for the time you've given me with Dad. You've even got Ryan helping me—even if it is just to keep his image. Thanks for giving me the opportunity to make this happen.* Amber crunched through the fall leaves. *My feelings wouldn't be hurt if the scrimmage got rained out tomorrow. Please, God, I don't want to disappoint my dad or my teammates. Do you think you could add rain to your plan? Amen.*

Saturday morning, Amber awoke to the patter of rain outside. "Yes!" Amber could hardly contain herself. "Thank you, God!"

"Amber!" Dad called. "I'm making you breakfast before your game. What would you like?" *Dad's home! I didn't even hear him come in last night.*

Amber tugged her robe tightly around her waist and skipped to the kitchen. She gave her dad a big hug. "It's raining!" Now they could stay home—watch old movies and play backgammon.

"Yep. You're going to love it!" Dad said. "Makes the game so much more challenging."

Amber felt her heart drop. "But the field will be all muddy, and we'll get soaking wet, and . . ."

"A little rain never stopped a soccer game," said Dad.

"Great." Amber opened the blinds and watched the rain pelt the lawn. She ate breakfast while her father related story after story about great rain games he had played in college.

By the time she and her dad got to the field, Amber's stomach hurt. *I'm bad enough when the ground is dry, let alone add mud.*

Amber slogged to her position alongside her teammates. The rain stuck her shorts to her thighs. A chill ran down her back as she waited.

The ref blew the whistle and the game began. Players slid everywhere—scrambling on the ground as much as they moved on their feet.

Whoosh! The ball splashed in front of her. Amber struggled to dribble, but the ball moved sluggishly with the tug of the soupy field. An opponent blocked her way, but Amber feinted the ball and kept shuffling toward the goal.

She watched as another opponent came at her fast. The girl slid, knocking Amber off her feet, and the ball rolled off for the taking. Samantha swooped in and kept the ball moving toward the goal. Sam kicked, and the team scored the first goal of the game.

A few die-hard fans in the bleachers huddled under big black umbrellas.

Bren's yellow Eddie Bauer umbrella bobbed up and down as she chanted cheer after cheer.

The team trudged on through the mud. The ball felt like it was filled with sand every time Amber had a chance to work it. But she managed to keep it in play. Suddenly, the ball flew to her. She looked down at a wide-open field and began dribbling. She could hear her teammates yelling.

I'm going to do it! I'm going to score a goal! Amber aimed and shot. *It went in! I scored a goal! I did it!* Amber jumped and turned to see the shocked faces of her teammates.

Sam grabbed Amber's arm. "You loser! You scored a goal for the other team!"

Amber's knees buckled under her, but the game went on. Amber felt like she was caught in quicksand—soon to suffocate.

Finally the mud bath ended. Her team had lost by three points. One of those points was hers. On the sidelines, Amber waited for the ax to fall.

"OK, girls. That was some interesting playing out there today," Mrs. Short said, shaking water from her rain poncho.

"I'll be posting the team on the bulletin board Monday, and the first game will be that same night. Enjoy the rest of your weekend."

Amber nodded. *Great. I get to worry about this for two more days.*

chapter.10

Squish! Squash! Squish! Squash! Amber's shoes made the only sound in the locker room as Sam and the others dressed silently. Amber could feel her teammates shooting her dirty looks. Holding back tears, she grabbed her bag and ran out.

"Wait up!" Sam shouted, tailing her.

Amber rounded the corner and crumpled onto the stairs. Sam was the last person she wanted to see. "I guess you're happy now," said Amber. "I proved myself to be the loser you knew I was."

Sam looked down at her. "You're hardly a loser."

Amber wiped her face on her wet shirt. She wasn't sure if she'd heard Sam right. "I scored for the other team!"

"Oh yeah, I forgot," said Sam. "Guess you are a big loser."

Amber squinted at Sam. "You're kidding, right?"

"Of course I'm kidding," said Sam. "Losers aren't usually swim team stars and Web masters, are they?"

Amber nodded. This was more like the old Sam—the one Amber knew before soccer. "But what do I say to my dad? He's my biggest fan."

Sam shook her head, splattering mud on the stairwell. "I know what you mean. I just got into the game to hang out with my dad more. But when I messed up on the field, I couldn't even look at him."

Amber wrapper her arms around her knees. "What am I going to say to him? He's waiting for me out in the car."

Sam shrugged. "Tell him you'll do better next time."

"If there is a next time." Amber sighed. "For all I know, I'll be off the list Monday."

"You were playing tight until that goal."

"You think?" Amber thought about Sam's dad, sitting in the bleachers by her own dad. "It's not easy raising dads, huh?" Amber squeezed the water out of her shirt.

"You got that right!" agreed Sam.

Amber headed for the truck. Dad sat behind the wheel, staring out the rain-streaked window. She climbed in and got goose bumps all over from the cold seats. Neither of them said a word.

"Dad . . ."

"Amber . . . ," Dad said.

"You go first." Amber grinned.

"You played a good game." Dad looked straight ahead.

Amber shifted in her seat. "Right up to the part when I scored for the other team."

Dad chuckled uneasily. "It happens even to the best players. I remember watching an international game. I believe it was Peru playing Britain—they were tied up, and this British forward pops that baby right into the wrong goal. Almost started a war right there on the field."

They were both quiet again. Amber hated the silence. She wanted to say she was sorry. Sorry for being such a lousy player. Sorry for kicking a goal for the other team. Sorry for disappointing him. But if she started, she'd burst out crying. And the last thing her dad needed was a lousy player who was also a crybaby. So she bit her lip and listened to the windshield wipers swish back and forth in front of her.

"Your dribbling was super." Dad started the engine. "Even with the water. And you feinted past your opponent."

Again, silence. "You're really lucky to have friends that would come in the pouring rain to watch you play. Jamie was there—and that Bren is really something, cheering away under her umbrella!"

Amber laughed. "All I could see was her umbrella popping up and down!"

Dad laughed, too. "You missed it. When Sam scored, Bren did some kind of cheer-jump, and she slipped and fell in the mud."

"No way!" Amber laughed at the thought of Bren coated with mud. "I bet she died! Bren hates dirt."

"Yeah, you could tell. She and Jamie headed home early." Dad wiped the windshield with his sleeve. "But I've got to hand it to them. They stuck in there most of the game." He pulled into the drive.

"Thanks for coming to the game, Dad," she said. "I'm sorry . . ." The words wouldn't go past the lump the size of a soccer ball in her throat.

"Nothing to be sorry for," Dad said. "Learn from your mistakes."

Amber showered, then got to work on the Web site. Hours later she heard the doorbell ring.

"Amber!" Ryan called. "Company."

Amber hit *Save* and ran to the front door to find Alex holding a tray of brownies.

"These are great," Ryan said inhaling one whole. "You made them?"

"Yeah." Alex held out the tray for Amber. "Go for it."

Amber shook her head. "No thanks."

"Well, you can bring me brownies any time you want." Ryan winked at Alex and disappeared into the kitchen with the whole tray.

"My grandmother thought your brother deserved brownies for helping the team." Alex dug into her right jacket pocket. "She sent you some Bible verses for the site."

"Cool!" Amber read through the list of verses.

James 1:2–3: My brothers, you will have many kinds of troubles. But when these things happen, you should be very happy. You know that these things are testing your faith. And this will give you patience.

2 Thessalonians 1:3: We must always thank God for you. And we should do this because it is right. It is right because your faith is growing more and more. And the love that every one of you has for each other is also growing.

Galatians 1:10: Do you think I am trying to make people accept me? No! God is the One I am trying to please. Am I trying to please men? If I wanted to please men, I would not be a servant of Christ.

"I can't believe she found these for me," Amber said.

"No big deal," Alex said, staring off. "You want to see if Ryan can work out with us?"

"Nah. I've had enough soccer for one day," Amber said. "You want to see what I've done on the school site so far?"

"Sure." Alex and Amber raced up the hardwood steps to Amber's room. Amber pulled a second chair over to the computer for Alex, and they clicked through the new Web pages. Vibrant colors flashed across the screen.

Alex shook her head. "Man, you've been busy. I didn't even know we had half these clubs."

"So? What do you think?" Amber asked.

"You kidding? You blew me out of the water!" Alex leaned back on the zebra-print vanity stool.

"Oh, I need to post a new verse for the day." Amber typed TodaysGirls.com in the location bar.

Alex was silent.

"I like the Thessalonians verse," said Amber and typed:

2 Thessalonians 1:3: We must always thank God for you. And we should do this because it is right. It is right because your faith is growing more and more. And the love that every one of you has for each other is also growing.

Don't forget to thank God for your friends. Life isn't always easy, but friends are pockets of God's love helping us along our way. They're warming rays of sunshine on rainy days and breezes of laughter when things get hot! Tell God thanks today!

Amber's mom knocked and then stuck her head in the door. "Alex, can you stay for dinner?"

"Thanks. But not this time," Alex said. "My grandfather's on a family dinner kick."

After dinner, Amber went back to work on the school Web site. When the phone rang, she picked it up on the first ring.

"Amber, listen to this!" Maya talked so loud Amber had to hold the phone away from her ear. "I'm eavesdropping on Morgan and Alex in the chat room. I told them I was signing off, but I stuck around. Ready? Here goes."

Maya read over the phone while Amber strained to catch every word.

TX2step: he winked @ me today, right in front of U no
who
jellybean: kewl!
TX2step: and he loved the brownies
jellybean: he loves more than your brownies! Ha!
TX2step: its great practicing w/him

Amber froze—brownies, practice . . . Alex's crush was on Ryan! Now it all made sense. *Alex didn't come by to help me. Alex came to see Ryan. That little fake! She's using me to get to my brother!*

"Amber?" Maya asked. "Are you still there?"

"What a big phony!" Amber paced while she talked. "All this time Alex has been building me up and coming over to help me with soccer." She kicked the soccer ball into the closet. "I believed her! She was just cozying up to me to get to Ryan!"

"I know!" said Maya. "Who does she think she is?"

"She even brought me Bible verses from her grandmother." Amber plopped down on her bed. "The new one I posted about friendship and faith was hers! She sat here while I wrote my Thought for the Day!"

"I read it," said Maya. "I assumed you meant me!"

"I should have used the Galatians verse." Amber began pacing again. "Talk about trying to make people accept you! Alex, the ultimate pleaser. All just so she could get what she wanted— my super dork brother!"

"What are you going to do?" Maya asked.

"I don't know," Amber said. "I am such a sucker."

"We have to teach Alex a lesson," Maya insisted.

Amber couldn't think straight. "I wouldn't know how to do that."

"Leave it to me," Maya said. "In the meantime, don't let on to Alex that you know. Chat starts in fifteen minutes. Just act natural."

"Whatever." Amber hung up. She replayed all the times she and Alex had practiced together, every two-faced, pseudo-word that came from Alex's mouth.

Amber stomped downstairs to get a bowl of ice cream. She chiseled out chunks of mint chocolate chip ice cream like she was breaking up concrete. She threw a spoon in the bowl and stormed back to her room for the chat.

How could she act like nothing was up?

rembrandt: sounds like U found some good buys

nycbutterfly: new red purse 2 match my coat

chicChick: i found 3 delicious pairs of earrings

rembrandt: the gnosh was packed

jellybean: some people have to work 4 a living

nycbutterfly: boo hoo! get over it

faithful1: Hi!

TX2step: hey! hows school site?

faithful1: getting there, and thanks for UR verses--TX
    helped me

nycbutterfly: Wow! i'm impressed
faithful1: i was 2
TX2step: my grandmother sent those

Amber took a deep breath. *Just like your grandmother asked you to make brownies?*

jellybean: U R the best 2step

It was all Amber could do not to type, "The best what?" *The best phony trying to please me to get to Ryan?*

faithful1: i'll B using UR other verses 2
TX2step: GR8: i can bring more 2 U

Yeah, you'd just love another reason to come over here, wouldn't you? Amber was fuming. *I better log off before I say something.*

faithful1: i have 2 get back 2 work--just wanted to say hi
nycbutterfly: hang in there . . . talk 2 U later

As soon as Amber logged out of the chat room, Maya called.

"Could you believe her?" Amber stared at her swim team photograph as she lay on her bed.

"Working you with Bible verses," said Maya. "She's sharp! But not as sharp as I am."

"I already have one idea," said Amber. "This is one of the other verses from her grandmother: Galatians 1:10: 'Do you think I am trying to make people accept me? No! God is the One I am trying to please. Am I trying to please men? If I wanted to please men, I would not be a servant of Christ.'

"So I thought I could hit her square between the eyes with that verse and my Thought for the Day."

"That is so you, Amber," said Maya. "Sure, you can hit her with a Bible verse, but I think we ought to do something with more bite. We should use the fact that she's priming you to get to Ryan."

"Like how?" asked Amber.

"I don't know yet," Maya said. "Maybe to frustrate her, you could make her keep running back and forth bringing you things when Ryan isn't around. Or maybe you could have her come a million times when he is around and let her give herself away."

"Yeah, but what if he falls for her?" Amber said. "Then she's gotten what she wanted by working me."

"No way!" said Maya. "Ryan couldn't care less about freshmen."

"But I want her to trap herself!" Amber insisted.

"What do you mean?" Maya asked.

"Well, I could write a note that says how great it's been getting to know her, spending time together, how she's a whiz at soccer, how I love her brownies, how thoughtful she is. See, all of that could come from Ryan or me. I'd end the letter with how much I'd love to have lunch with her on Monday and would she please come sit by me."

"I don't get it," Maya said.

"I'm not going to sign the letter," Amber said. She hadn't actually formed the plan until that minute. "Alex will give herself away as soon as she sits down."

"And if she sits with Ryan and his friends, he'll freak! What a great setup!" Maya squealed. "She traps herself! Amber, girl, I didn't know you had it in you!"

Amber felt a twinge of guilt, but she stuffed it with righteous indignation. Alex betrayed her trust. And besides, Alex would be the one to seal her own fate.

"Well," said Amber, "it's time that freshman realizes she can't get what she wants by trying to please her way into people's lives."

chapter.11

Sunday morning Amber and her family arrived at church early. Amber sat in her family's pew, lost in the quiet. She breathed deeply and closed her eyes, imaging her worries flowing out of her with each exhale.

God, please let me make the school proud of the Web site, and please don't let me embarrass my dad by being kicked off the soccer team. Thank you for always giving me the peace only you can give.

She hated for the service to end. For the first time in her life, she didn't want to have to talk with anyone afterward. Instead of heading outside, she let her purse drop and dump open, sprawling the contents on the floor and under the pew. She slowly picked up each item piece by piece, watching as the church emptied out.

Amber stood up, breathing in the blended smell of flowers and candles, and then left the stained-glass light for the fall sky outside. She stopped on the church steps. Her father was talk-ing with Mrs. Short while her husband chased after their boys.

She's telling him I'm off the team. He's begging her to let me stay. Amber's mind raced. She hurried over to them. "Didn't you love the hymns today, Mrs. Short?"

She smiled. Amber noticed how nice she looked with her hair down. "We sang some of my favorites," Mrs. Short answered. "Well, I should save Harry from the boys."

"They're sure growing up fast," Dad said.

"Yeah, especially Harrison Sr.!" She smiled as Coach climbed the jumbo-gym.

Dad laughed, and Amber sighed in relief.

"Your coach told me what a help Ryan's been with the soccer team," Dad said as they joined Mom and walked to the car.

Mrs. Short was talking about Ryan. She doesn't want to give Dad the bad news. She wants to leave that to me. Great. I don't know which is worse.

Dad and Ryan talked all the way home about Ryan's escapades on the field training the rookies.

When they got home, she checked her e-mail and found sev-enteen messages adding last-minute requests for the school site. She dashed off a group reply:

Dear All--

Thank you for your interest in the school Web site. I appreciate your suggestions and will try to incorporate your requests. The site will be officially up on Monday the twenty-third. I hope you're happy with the results.

    The site will continually be updated, so if you don't see your suggestions on the initial viewing, know that we'll be working on it daily to make it the best.

Your Web master,
Amber Thomas

She reread the message before hitting *Send*. Then she took a closer look at the suggestions. She could only include a couple of them on such short notice. *I just hope everyone will understand and love the final site.* She worked through the day and long into the night.

At midnight her dad came in. "You need to call it a night."

Amber rubbed her eyes. "Yeah, I'm about finished."

"I'm impressed with how hard you've worked on this site," Dad said, looking over her shoulder. "I hope the school realizes how much time you've put into this thing."

Amber yawned. "Thanks, Dad."

"I love you, pumpkin. Good night."

"Love you too, Dad."

The next morning Amber did a quick update on her verse and Thought for the Day.

Galatians 1:10: Do you think I am trying to make people accept me? No! God is the One I am trying to please. Am I trying to please men? If I want to please men, I would not be a servant of Christ.

She knew without thinking what she wanted to write for her Thought for the Day.

Pleasing people can only backfire on you because people fail you. On the other hand, pleasing God rocks. Ask yourself: Am I trying to please people or God?

Amber hitched an early ride with Coach Short and Jamie. She wanted to run though the Web site with Mr. Baldwin one last time before it went live.

"What's up with Maya?" Jamie asked in the van. "I saw her last night, and she seemed really preoccupied."

Amber hesitated then decided she could confide in Jamie and Coach.

"You know how Alex has been helping and encouraging me with soccer? And her grandmother sent me the Bible verses for the site? It turns out Alex was just pretending to be my friend so she could get her hooks into Ryan."

For a minute no one said anything. Then Jamie asked, "Are you sure? I mean maybe—"

"No maybe about it!" Amber insisted, wondering if Alex had been using Jamie, too.

"It's just," Jamie said, "she's not as full of attitude at the Gnosh."

"That's hardly the same thing," Amber insisted. "Believe me. I know what I'm talking about. She's got a huge crush on Ryan. She was acting friendly just to get on my good side."

Coach glanced over at her. "You know, Amber, Alex has come a long way since she moved here from Texas. She used to go out of her way not to please anybody. Not that I'm saying she needs to please us—God's the only one we ought to try to please."

"I know!" Amber said. "I actually posted a verse that says that."

Coach Short pulled into the parking lot. "Well, I wish you all would just try to get along. If you want me to talk to Alex, I . . ."

"That's OK, Coach," Amber said quickly. "I've got it covered."

Jamie and Coach walked to the pool, and Amber headed for the computer lab, passing Alex's locker on the way. She pulled the note out of her pocket and slipped it into the top slot on the locker door. She pushed it halfway in and then hesitated.

Would this please God? Amber shook off the thought. *This is an invitation to join me for lunch. That's all. Alex will choose who she wants to sit with.* Amber pushed the note all the way in and then hurried to the computer lab.

Amber switched on the computer and waited for it to boot up.

"Good morning, Amber!" Mr. Baldwin bellowed as he set down his briefcase. "This is your big day!"

"Boy, am I glad to see you," she said. "I really wanted to run this whole thing past you before we go live this morning."

"Feeling butterflies?" Mr. Baldwin asked, crossing the room to her computer.

"Yeah, I guess," Amber said. "I just want everyone to like the site."

"OK. Let's take a look at what you've got." He pulled up a chair next to her.

They viewed the site, starting with the home page and ending with the alumni pages.

Amber waited for Mr. Baldwin's response. He sat with his lips pursed and arms crossed.

"So?" Amber asked impatiently. "You hate it?"

"No," Mr. Baldwin said. "Not at all! I'm just astonished with what a good job you did in such a short amount of time."

"You mean it?" she asked, feeling her neck muscles begin to relax.

"Really!" Mr. Baldwin said. "I don't think I could have done a better job myself."

Amber grinned. "Thanks. I needed to hear that."

She still had to go by the girls' locker room to see if Mrs. Short had posted the soccer team results yet. She'd have to scoot to get to first block before announcements. The tension in her neck returned, and she tried to blow it off.

"See you later, Mr. Baldwin." She grabbed her bag and rushed to the locker room. *Please, please let me make the team.* She raced through the crowded hallways. Bren called out her name. Amber waved but didn't slow down. "I can't stop! I've got to get to the locker room and back before homeroom."

Inside the locker room, a couple of girls crowded around the bulletin board. Amber held her breath as she edged her way up and read the list of soccer team members: Sam, Alex, Heather, Trisha, Morgan, Andrea. Amber's heart pounded. Molly, Kelsey . . . She kept reading. Finally, she saw her name, the last one. *I made it! I didn't get kicked off!*

Sam came up behind Amber. "See, you're not a total loser."

Amber turned around and smiled. "I made it."

"Yeah," said Sam. "But you were last choice."

"That's just 'cause you make me look bad," said Amber. "See you in Spanish?"

"*Si,*" answered Sam.

Amber tried to collect herself. *I made the team. Last or not, I made the team. If I keep trying, I'll get better. I'll make Dad proud.* She headed out of the locker room. The halls still boiled with people.

"Hail! Almighty Web master!" Zack caught up with her outside the office. "Isn't this your big day?"

Amber grinned. Just looking at that handsome face erased all worries from her mind. Zack was just what she needed. "Hi, Zack. Walk me to class?"

"I'd be honored." Zack put out his arm for her. Amber felt like a total princess. "Did you get those wonderful pictures of the star football players on the Web site?" he asked.

"I think you'll be pleased," said Amber. She'd only had time to load four team pictures, but they'd turned out great.

They slipped into Spanish and, as usual, sat down just as the buzzer sounded. The morning announcements began. Mr. Carson stood in front of a computer smiling at the room from the TV screen.

"Good morning!" Mr. Carson boomed. "We will be following an early release schedule today."

"Yea!" Amber's classmates erupted.

"So we can unveil the new school Web site. All students will report back to homeroom after last block."

The class groaned. Amber shifted in her seat. A kid in the back of the room said, "Man, what a tease! Doesn't early release mean we get out of here?"

Zack spoke up. "Hey! It's gonna be great!" He winked at Amber.

Amber smiled back. "Thanks."

Spanish and computer lab flew by in a blur. Amber kept running through the different Web site pages in her mind, hoping she hadn't forgotten anything. By the time she sat down with Maya at lunch, Amber's mind was a million miles away.

"It's zero hour," Maya said.

Amber looked at Maya, confused. "What?"

"Alex is in the lunch line." Maya practically sang as she pointed.

All of a sudden, Amber felt like someone had awakened her from a sound sleep. She glanced over at Alex, who was picking up two cookies and paying the cashier. Then she glanced at Ryan's table. Ryan and his friends were laughing and talking.

Alex looked like she had actually put some thought into what she was wearing today, unlike her usual grunge attire. She had on a sky-blue sweater, jeans, and even a little makeup.

Amber made a space next to her for Alex to sit. In her heart, she hoped Alex wouldn't even look in Ryan's direction, but would come and sit by her. Alex scanned the lunchroom. Amber stood up and smiled over at her.

"Amber!" Maya pulled on Amber's sleeve. "Sit down! You're going to ruin everything!"

Amber plopped back in her seat. Alex never even looked in her direction. She walked right over to Ryan's table. Amber stared as Alex scooted in next to Ryan. His mouth dropped open as Alex handed him a cookie. Amber could read her brother's body language loud and clear.

Then the table of boys went wild. "Ryan's got a girlfriend!" Mike, Ryan's best friend chanted.

"Where's my cookie?" Jacob shouted over the lunchroom drone. "I need a girlfriend to bring me cookies!"

Alex seemed to ignore the guys and focused on Ryan.

Ryan burst out laughing and scooted away from Alex.

Watching Alex's face go from smiling, to confused, to hurt, then angry was like watching a morph scene in a sci-fi movie. And Amber knew she was the one who had written the script.

Alex flew out of her seat and ran out of the lunchroom.

Maya held out her fist to knock against Amber's, but Amber couldn't. "Come on, girl!" Maya grinned. "You got her!"

Amber bit the inside of her lip. "She did it to herself." Amber wanted to believe what she was saying, but her heart told her differently. Jamie and Bren walked up and climbed over the bench across from Maya.

"Hey, Amber, I can't wait to see the Web site!" Bren said. "Aren't you excited? Everybody's talking about it, even the Dragon Lady. Did you really put up a picture of her? And how did our cheerleaders' pyramid turn out?"

Amber tried to swallow the bite of peanut butter sandwich that seemed to have lodged itself in her throat. "Sure."

"What's with you?" Bren cried. "I thought you'd be psyched."

Amber took a swig of her milk. "Nervous, I guess," she stammered, glad Bren couldn't read minds.

"I hear that," Jamie said, digging into her spaghetti. "I always feel that way about showing my artwork."

"Your artwork rocks!" Bren exclaimed. "I can't imagine stressing about it! I wish I had half the talent you have. And

Amber! You're the Web princess! The school site is going to rock!"

"Always the cheerleader!" Maya teased.

"Looks like you need a cheerleader here!" Bren flipped her hair.

"Wonder where Alex and Morgan are today," Jamie said, surveying the room. Amber looked to Maya.

"Morgan had a student council meeting," Maya said.

Amber stood. "I have to get going." She had to get away and think.

"But you haven't finished your lunch," Bren said.

"Guess I'm too nervous to eat." Amber dumped her tray and left the lunchroom.

She ran to the bathroom looking for Alex, but she wasn't there. She jogged to the locker room and the pool, but still didn't find Alex. Amber felt the guilt spreading through her like a flu virus.

When students asked about the Web site, Amber just nodded, feeling as though she were watching a movie of herself: moving, talking, responding. She didn't hear a word of her English lecture. When the final buzzer sounded, everyone reported to homeroom. Amber felt like she'd been hit by the Concorde.

Senor Vasquez turned on the TV monitor in front of the class. Mr. Carson was on the screen again, standing in front of a computer. "Today is a momentous day for Edgewood High

School." He sat down next to the computer screen. "I am proud to say we are embarking on the computer age with our very own Web site, thanks to the hard work of our Web master, Amber Thomas."

The class clapped. Amber smiled, drumming the desk as the camera zeroed in on the computer monitor that showed the home page. Amber glanced around the room to see her class-mates' responses.

Senor Vasquez was the first to speak. "Looks good, Amber."

"How come nothing's moving?" Molly asked. "I thought our home page would look jazzier."

"I've done pages with movement," Amber said. "I just thought the home page should be straightforward."

Mr. Carson revealed the school site page by page. And as each page was revealed, someone in the class had a complaint.

"The theater page just is not avant-garde!" said Lindsay. At least she didn't wave her arms around as much this time.

"I thought you were going to have a sound clip for the debate club," Heather griped.

But the worst complaint of all came from Zack. "Hey, what happened to all the ideas you said you were going to include on the football pages?"

Amber's eyes filled. All her hard work. Everything she had done to try to please everyone had blown up in her face. They hated the Web site.

chapter.12

This is just the initial setup. I'll keep updating the site and incorporating your ideas." Amber held back the tears.

"I think you did a great job," Senor Vasquez said, moving back to his desk. "And we look forward to seeing the site grow. Now, let's give Amber a hand for all her hard work."

Amber looked around the room as her classmates clapped halfheartedly. She took a deep breath and held her head high. *I'm not gonna let them see me cry.* She forced a smile.

The buzzer sounded. Amber scooped up her bag and dashed for the door.

"Amber!" Senor Vasquez called. "What's the rush?"

"I have to get to soccer. We have our first game tonight." Amber felt like she couldn't breathe.

"OK." Senor Vasquez nodded. "We'll talk tomorrow."

Amber's heart pounded so hard she could hear it in her head. She flew into the safety of the locker room, dumped her bag on the floor, and collapsed crying. *I'm a failure! Everyone, every club, every team, and all the teachers think I'm a big loser. They hate the Web site!*

Suddenly, Alex came out of nowhere. "You!"

Amber backed up to a locker.

"You set me up!" Alex's face was red and swollen from crying.

"You set yourself up!" Amber shouted back. "You played me to get to my brother! You're nothing but a phony!"

"You should talk, Miss High and Mighty!" Alex cried. "The only reason you're playing soccer is to please your dad! Talk about phonies. I've watched you try to please the whole school over this stupid Web site. Talk about kiss-ups! I'd say you're the ultimate!"

Amber felt like she had been slapped. *Me? How can she say I'm the phony?*

"What's wrong?" Alex sneered. "Can't stand the truth?" Alex slammed the locker next to Amber. "Isn't there something in the Bible about judging others?"

Amber knew the verse. Matthew 7:1. She whispered the words, "You will be judged in the same way that you judge others."

"Condemned by your own words." Alex left the locker room.

Is she right? Have I been so busy trying to please people I forgot about pleasing God? She wiped her face.

What was so wrong about wanting Dad to be proud of me? I wanted to be a soccer star for him, not myself.

And what about the Web site? I was just trying to do a good job.

Amber knew she wasn't being completely honest with herself. *OK, so I was trying to do a good job—but why? for God?*

Morgan flew through the door. She was already dressed out. "I've been looking for you."

Amber braced herself for another attack.

"I just saw Alex," Morgan said, her eyes welling up. "She's really upset, Amber. Alex wasn't being a fake. Honest. Sure, she admits she likes Ryan and wanted to be around him. But last week she told me how cool it was getting to know you."

The tears spilled down Amber's face. "I was so hurt when I found out Alex was after Ryan, Morgan." Amber shook her head. "I told myself setting her up was fair because she was only using me to get to him."

Morgan got Amber some toilet paper to wipe her nose. "You'll find a way to make it right." Amber blew her nose and washed her face.

Morgan patted Amber on the back. "Come on. We have a game to play."

Out on the field, the team stretched, then jogged and dribbled. The crisp air felt good. Amber and Morgan joined in until Mrs. Short called the team together. Amber tried to make eye contact with Alex, but Alex's puffy eyes stayed focused on Mrs. Short.

"Sam, you're our center forward. Alex, you're inside right forward." Mrs. Short assigned the positions, going through position by position until she called Amber's name. "Amber, right side halfback."

Alex rolled her eyes. She finally looked at Amber. Amber mouthed, "Sorry," but Alex looked away.

Mrs. Short called the team huddle. "Now get out there and make me proud!"

The team scattered for their positions. Amber ran up next to Alex. "I'm sorry. But we both did things that weren't so great." It hadn't come out the way she meant. "What I'm trying to say is, I'd like to give our friendship another try."

Alex didn't say anything, and Amber had to hurry to her position. The whistle blew, and the game leaped into action. Amber looked into the stands to see Dad, Mom, and Ryan cheering, "Go Edgewood!"

Amber moved with her team up and down the field. Then it happened. The forward from the other team dribbled right toward her. Amber watched the ball roll closer and closer. All she had to do was tackle the ball. But her feet wouldn't move. She froze.

Alex blew past her and tackled the ball, bringing it back toward their goal.

Sam ran up next to Amber. "Sorry, but wake up, or get off the field! This game's for real."

Amber fumbled forward. She glanced at her dad. His gaze followed Alex as she passed the ball to Morgan. Morgan aimed and shot. The goalie caught the ball and kicked it back out to the field. Alex retrieved the ball and passed it to Sam, who kicked it back. Alex shot the ball low and deep. Score!

Mrs. Short called Amber to the sidelines and replaced her

with Haley. "What's going on out there, Amber? You look like a bundle of nerves."

"I know. I stink," Amber admitted.

"Not during practices, you don't," Mrs. Short said. "I've seen what you're capable of. For some reason, you fall apart when you have to compete. What's that about?"

"I don't want to embarrass my dad," Amber mumbled.

Mrs. Short put her hand on Amber's shoulder. "Amber, it's OK not to be great. Play because you enjoy the game, not because your dad does."

Amber nodded but couldn't stand to think of Dad being disappointed.

"If you think you can give yourself a break and play because you want to, I'll put you back in. If not, then you should think about quitting the team."

Quit the team! Amber looked over to where her father sat. He jumped up, cheering for her teammates.

Mrs. Short turned her attention back to the game, and Amber dropped down on the bench. She held her head in her hands. Behind her, she could hear Dad cheering.

Dear heavenly Father, she prayed. *Please forgive me for messing up so much. I can't please everybody—I see that now. This feels just like when I first became a Christian and thought I could earn your love. You taught me about your grace. You love me unconditionally. All I can do is try my best and leave the rest up to you, God.*

Amber felt like a huge weight had been lifted off her shoulders. She looked up just in time to see Morgan kick a goal. The team surrounded Morgan with congratulations.

Amber shouted, "Way to go, Morgan!" She sprinted down the sidelines to Mrs. Short. "Mrs. Short, please let me play."

"You think you can go in and give yourself a break?" she asked.

Amber grinned and nodded. She raced back on the field and ran with her teammates, following the ball. But this time she wasn't hoping the ball would stay away from her. Instead she cheered as Haley made a steal, passing the ball to Sam, who made a clear shot to Amber. Amber received the ball with her chest, rolling it down to her feet.

Yes! She dribbled the ball as an opponent came in for a tackle. Amber side-kicked the ball to Alex. Alex and Amber worked together getting the ball downfield closer and closer to the goal. Two feet in front of the goal, Alex passed back to Amber. But instead of shooting, Amber passed the ball back to Alex. Alex had a clear shot to the goal. She looked at Amber. Amber smiled. Alex aimed, shot, and scored!

"We did it!" Alex slammed both fists with Amber.

"You did it," said Amber. "If you hadn't helped me, I'd still be scoring goals for the other team!"

All of a sudden, Alex was surrounded by her teammates congratulating her.

Amber returned to her position. She played soccer like she never had before, filled with a joy and an enthusiasm that came from the freedom of being set free.

The final score was Edgewood 9, Norton 7. The spectators flooded the field to congratulate the team on their first win.

"Way to go, Amber!" Dad hugged her tightly.

"Thanks." Amber smiled up at him.

Ryan nudged Amber's head. "Yeah, you actually played like a real soccer player."

Amber punched his arm. "Must have been all that practice."

"Yeah," said Ryan. "The Thomas touch!"

"Alex played a good game, don't you think?" Amber stared at her brother.

"Yeah. She scored the most points," he said, a crooked smile on his lips.

Amber elbowed him. "Maybe you ought to congratulate her."

She watched as Ryan walked up to Alex. At first Alex looked flustered. But as Ryan continued to talk, Amber could see Alex slowly relax. Amber realized she'd been holding her own breath, too.

Dad came back from congratulating Sam and Morgan on their game and put his arm around Amber. "It was good to see you finally relax and enjoy the game today."

Amber stared at her dad. "What do you mean?"

"Well, up until today you've always looked like a fish out of water. But today you seemed to flow. I was glad to see you get into the game like I used to."

Amber hugged her father. Nothing he could have said would have pleased her more.

Epilogue

Later that night Amber checked her school Web site e-mail and found more than one hundred hits on the site. She began opening each message with apprehension. But as she scrolled through the messages one by one, the majority congratulated her on a job well done. There were still several complaints, but Amber could deal with that now. She knew she couldn't please everyone—ever—no matter how hard she tried.

For the congratulations, Amber wrote a quick note of thanks. And for the criticism, she wrote:

Dear Fellow Student--
    Thanks for making me aware of your concern. I will consider your input and make suggested changes where I feel it will better the site and when time

allows. My purpose as a Web master is to make the best possible site to represent the school as a whole.

Your Web master,
Amber

Amber clicked over to the TodaysGirls chat room.

faithful1: what a day!

nycbutterfly: told you ya were a soccer star

faithful1: nope, that's 2step

TX2step: thanx, I try

jellybean: what about me?

nycbutterfly: u2 little sister

rembrandt: anybody hear us cheering today?

chicChick: man2man, girl2girl, if edgewood loses, im gonna hurl

TX2step: Please no more!

rembrandt: bicycle, banana, peppermint clump. if you're not for edgewood, you're a chump!

nycbutterfly: whats a peppermint clump?

chicChick: I don't know. it rhymed with chump.

faithful1: I think it's that glob of hard candy thats always stuck @ the bottom of ur grandma's candy dish

The phone rang just as Amber hit *Enter.* Her mom's voice called up the stairs, "Amber, phone."

"OK," Amber called back. She keyed in, "BRB" then picked up the receiver in her room. "Hello?" It was Zack!

"Sorry about being a toad about the football page," said Zack. "You really did a great job."

"Thanks," said Amber. She smiled into the phone.

"Good game today, too," added Zack. "I was really impressed." Amber typed in a quick message to her girlfriends:

faithful1: Zack's on the phone!!! gotta go!

nycbutterfly: call me next! I wanna know everything!

chicChick: Zack! Zack! He's so fine. He likes Amber. That's no line!

TX2step: enuf!

Net Ready, Set, Go!

I hope my words and thoughts please you.
Psalm 19:14

The characters of TodaysGirls.com chat online in the safest—and maybe most fun—of all chat rooms! They've created their own private Web site and room! Many Christian teen sites allow you to create your own private chat rooms, and there are other safe options.

Work with your parents to develop a list of safe, appropriate chat rooms. Earn Internet freedom by showing them you can make the right choices. *Honor your father and your mother (Deuteronomy 5:16).*

Before entering a chat room, you'll select a user name. Although you can use your real name, a nickname is safer. Most people choose one that says something about who they are, like Amber's name, faithful1. Don't be discouraged if the name you select is already taken. You can use a similar one by adding a number at its end.

No one will notice your grammar in a chat room. Don't worry if you spell something wrong or forget to capitalize. Some people even misspell words on purpose. You might see a sentence like How R U?

But sometimes it's important to be accurate. Web site and e-mail addresses must be exact. Pay close attention to whether letters are upper- or lowercase. Remember that Web site addresses don't use some punctuation marks, such as hyphens and apostrophes. (That's why the "Today's" in TodaysGirls.com has no apostrophe!) And instead of using spaces between words, underlines are used to_make_the_spaces. And sometimes words just run together like onebigword.

When you're in a chat room, remember that real people are typing the words that appear on your screen. Treat them with the same respect you expect from them. Don't say anything you wouldn't want repeated in Sunday school. *Do for other people what you want them to do for you (Luke 6:31).*

Sometimes people say mean, hurtful things—things that make us angry. This can happen in chat rooms, too. In some chat rooms, you can highlight a rude person's name and click a button that says, "ignore," which will make his or her comments disappear from your screen. You always have the option to switch rooms or sign off. If a particular person becomes a continual problem, or if someone says something especially vicious, you should report this problem user to the chat service. *Ask God to bless those who say bad things to you. Pray for those who are cruel (Luke 6:28–29).*

Remember that Internet information is not always factual. Whether you're chatting or surfing Web sites, be skeptical about information and people. Not everything on the Internet is true. You don't have to be afraid of the Internet, but you should always be cautious. Practice caution with others even in Christian chat rooms.

It's okay to chat about your likes and dislikes, but *never* give out personal information. Do not tell anyone your name, phone number, address, or even the name of your school, team, church, or neighborhood. Be cautious . . . *You will be like sheep among wolves. So be as smart as snakes. But also be like doves and do nothing wrong. Be careful of people (Matthew 10:16–17).*

STRANGER ONLINE

AMBER
THOMAS

16/junior
e-name: faithful1
best friend: Maya
site area: Thought for the Day

Confident. Caring. Swimmer. Single-handedly built
TodaysGirls.com Web site. Loves her folks.
Big brother Ryan drives her nuts! Great friend.
Got a problem? Go to Amber.

JAMIE CHANDLER

PORTRAIT OF LIES

15/sophomore
e-name: rembrandt
best friend: Bren
site area: Artist's Corner

Quiet. Talented artist. Works at the Gnosh Pit
after school. Dad left when she was little.
Helps her mom with younger sisters Jordan and
Jessica. Baby-sits for Coach Short's kids.

ALEX DIAZ

TANGLED WEB

14/freshman
e-name: TX2step
best friend: Morgan
site area: to be determined . . .

Spicy. Hot-tempered Texan. Lives with grandparents because
of parents' problems. Won state in freestyle swimming at her
old school. Snoops. Into everything. Breaks the rules.

R U 4 REAL?

16/junior
e-name: nycbutterfly
best friend: Amber
site area: What's Hot—What's Not
(under construction)

MAYA CROSS

Fashion freak. Health nut. Grew up in New York City.
Small town drives her crazy. Loves to dance.
Dad owns the Gnosh Pit. Little sis Morgan is also
a TodaysGirl.

BREN MICKLER

LUV@FIRST SITE

15/sophomore
e-name: chicChick
best friend: Jamie
site area: Smashin' Fashion (under construction)

Funny. Popular. Outgoing. Spaz. Cheerleader. Always late.
Only child. Wealthy family. Bren is chatting—
about anything, online and off, except when
she's eating junk food.

CHAT FREAK

14/freshman
e-name: jellybean
best friend: Alex
site area: Feeling All Write

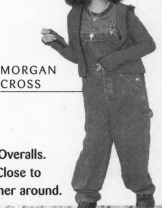

MORGAN
CROSS

The Web-ster. Spends too much time online. Overalls.
M&M's. Swim team. Tries to save the world. Close to
her family—when her big sister isn't bossing her around.

Cyber Glossary

Bounced mail An e-mail that has been returned to its sender.

Chat A live conversation, typed or spoken through microphones, among individuals in a chat room.

Chat room A "place" on the Internet where individuals meet to "talk" with one another.

Crack To break a security code.

Download To receive information from a more powerful computer.

E-mail Electronic mail that is sent through the Internet.

E-mail address An Internet address where e-mail is received.

File Any document or image stored on a computer.

Floppy disk A small, thin, plastic object that stores information to be accessed by a computer.

Hacker Someone who tries to gain unauthorized access to another computer or network of computers.

Header Text at the beginning of an e-mail that identifies the sender, subject matter, and the time at which it was sent.

Home page A Web site's first page.

Internet A worldwide electronic network that connects computers to one another.

Link Highlighted text or a graphic element that may be clicked with the mouse in order to "surf" to another Web site or page.

Log on/Log in To connect to a computer network.

Modem A device that enables computers to exchange information.

Net, the The Internet.

Newbie A person who is learning or participating in something new.

Online To have Internet access. Can also mean to use the Internet.

Surf To move from page to page through links on the Web.

Upload To send information to a more powerful computer.

Web, the The World Wide Web or WWW.